Rawhide: Ace in the Hole

by

Desiree Holt

Rawhide: Ace in the Hole

Contact Information: info@thewildrosepress.com

Cover Art by *Diana Carlile*

The Wild Rose Press, Inc.
PO Box 708
Adams Basin, NY 14410-0708

Visit us at www.thewildrosepress.com

Publishing History
First Scarlet Rose Edition, 2021
Trade Paperback ISBN 978-1-5092-3482-0
Digital ISBN 978-1-5092-3483-7

Published in the United States of America

Dedication

To Laura Topaz, who gave me the
idea for this fabulous anthology,
and to my endlessly patient,
wonderful editor, Diana Carlile.

Dear Readers,

Welcome back to Rawhide, the exclusive high-end, sought-after BDSM club in San Antonio, Texas. It's been a while since we visited there, but here we are and with some new characters. For one thing, the club has added a Dungeon Master, a mysterious but knowledgeable man known only as Ruelas. For another, our new cast of characters includes Doms with an anguished history and brand new subs exploring their newly realized submissive sides. So put on your best halters, short skirts, and thigh-high boots and join us at Rawhide, where your wildest fantasies can come true.

Then please join us at Desiree's Darlings, where we celebrate and discuss all my books, and every day is a party.

https://www.facebook.com/groups/DesireesDarlings

Desiree
XOXO

Cut the Cards

"Welcome to Rawhide, Miss LeBlanc." Clint Chavez, a partner in the premier BDSM club, Rawhide, smiled and nodded. "Reulas will be pleased you were able to make it tonight."

"His email sounded exciting. Something new. How could I resist? In fact, I'm looking forward to it." Kelly LeBlanc held out her hand. "May I have a key, please?"

"Of course." He lifted one from a board set into a recess on the wall. "Your usual locker is available."

She shrugged out of her thin coat. "It isn't often I get a special call from the new Dungeon Master, asking for my presence. Or my participation in a special event. A demonstration, he said?"

Clint smiled. "We are introducing a new activity tonight. I believe he thinks you are the perfect sub for it."

"A performance?" She lifted an eyebrow. "I haven't done one in a while."

"Reulas knows what he's doing. You quickly became one of his favorites."

She knew that. She also had a feeling the Dom involved with the demonstration would be hardcore.

For some time now, the Doms she'd been playing with hadn't really fulfilled her needs. More and more, she wanted someone to push her past one edge and then another. She'd talked to Reulas about the ramping up of her needs, told him about the extremes she now wanted from her Doms.

Reulas, being the careful person he was, had questioned her until he was assured she knew what she wanted and needed. Satisfied, he'd told her he'd take care of her. Maybe this was his idea of giving her what she'd asked for. Kelly trusted him, knew he wouldn't put her with anyone who was too over the top. Still, he had acknowledged her need for a more demanding Dom, a more inventive one.

Clint nodded toward the cloakroom. "I'd put my things away. Reulas doesn't like to be kept waiting, even for someone special." Then he surprised her with a conspiratorial wink. "He listened to what you said to him and set this up. But be prepared. We have a very large crowd tonight."

Kelly smoothed down her short, red leather skirt, adjusted the fabric of her abbreviated halter top also in screaming red, gave her long, blonde hair one last flip, and strode toward the main lounge on her stiletto thigh-high boots. She paused at the end of the short hall just as it widened into the lounge and took a long look.

It was indeed crowded tonight. Every table, every couch and chair was filled. Even the bar stools were all occupied. An air of excitement shimmered like electricity in the room.

Nodding and smiling at some familiar faces, she looked around for a place she might sit, wondering if someone would tell her what was on the schedule.

"Thank you so much for accepting my request for this evening," Reulas greeted her. The Dungeon Master was a man of mystery. No one really knew where he'd come from or how he'd ended up at Rawhide.

Kelly had been a member for five years and was known by the regulars as someone who chose her Doms very carefully. She never played with a certain one for too long, but she had a reputation for being responsive and sexually satisfying. She had her pick of Masters. That she was chosen for whatever was on tonight's agenda excited her, made her nipples tighten and her pussy throb in anticipation. Knowing Reulas, it was sure to be something that would appeal to her complicated needs.

"Allow me to introduce a very special friend of mine." He stepped to the side. "Kelly LeBlanc, meet Tanner Sloat."

At this point in her life, it took a lot to steal Kelly's breath, but the man with Reulas managed to do it in an instant. He wasn't as tall as most of the men she played with, probably not more than five ten, which suited her petite frame just fine. But it was a well-defined, sexually sizzling five foot ten. His body was muscular, not gym-conditioned, but that of a man who did some kind of hard labor for a living. Midnight-black hair hung in a thick curtain of silk just to his shoulders, and matching hair dusted the hard wall of his chest. His eyes were an unusual pale gray, fringed with thick black lashes, silver beacons in a square-jawed face with high cheekbones.

Tanner Sloat was everything subs imagined Doms to be, power flowing from his body. It was hard to ignore the bulge at his crotch, and it had cream flooding the tiny crotch of her thong at the sight of it. Her nipples hardened, poking into the soft material of her halter. At once, she imagined herself on her knees in front of him, his cock on her tongue, her hands

3

squeezing his balls. Would he spank her if he thought her performance lacking?

Oh, yes! Please!

She was instantly even more wet and needy, and he hadn't even said hello to her yet.

When she looked up at Tanner, a tiny knowing smile flirted with the corners of his mouth and sexual hunger flared in his eyes. He raked his gaze over her slowly, taking in every inch of her. Now she knew what the phrase "undressing someone with his eyes" meant, because that was exactly how she felt. At that moment, if he'd told her to strip naked, get down on her hands and knees, and let him fuck her ass, she'd have done it without a moment's hesitation.

Holy shit!

She swallowed and curved her mouth in a smile. "Welcome to Rawhide."

He dipped his head once. "I can see you're everything Reulas said you were."

And exactly what was that?

"Tanner is just back from a tour of duty as a member of a Delta Force team," Reulas explained.

Ooo-kay. So that explained the ripped body. She wondered if he had any interesting scars. Without realizing it, Kelly licked her lips.

"I picked up a little game while I was in...a different country," Tanner said. "When I mentioned it to Reulas, it interested him. He suggested giving a little presentation to the members." His eyes looked her over again. "From everything he told me, I thought you would be an excellent choice for a game partner. You enjoy exhibitionism, right?"

Did a bank have money? Heat sizzled through her

at the idea of performing before this crowd with this highly sexual man.

"I do," she answered. "Can you tell me what the game is about?"

He held out a deck of cards. "Take a look at these. The idea is each partner goes through the deck and removes any position or activity that they absolutely will not do. Then they go through them one at a time."

"Of course, no one expects to complete the entire selection in one session," Reulas added. "So each partner picks his or her top three and then they begin."

Kelly cocked an eyebrow at him. "Your email sounded intriguing, and everyone is always looking for something new. I'm sure that's why there's such a big crowd tonight."

Reulas nodded. "If I'd told them you were going to be part of the performance, we'd have been so crowded the fire marshal might have shut us down."

"Reulas tells me you are a particular favorite." Tanner's voice rolled over her nerves like the electric wand she loved so much, sending sparks along the surface of her skin.

"He's very kind. But I do my best to please."

"As a good sub should." He gave her a penetrating look that pierced all the way to her pussy. Her inner walls clenched, and she had to resist the urge to squeeze her thighs together.

"Why don't the two of you step into the little alcove over there?" Reulas pointed. "You can select your cards. When you're ready, I'll get everyone's attention and announce the beginning of the performance."

If Tanner hadn't come vetted by Reulas, Kelly

might have had second thoughts about this. She was very selective with her Doms, but the club owner wouldn't put her with a man unless he trusted him. Besides, she couldn't remember the last time she'd felt such a strong sexual pull, such a desire to do anything and everything with anyone, no restrictions.

She smiled at Tanner and waited for him to precede her, following him with her head down and hands clasped behind her back, already in her submissive role.

The alcove was barely more than a niche in the wall as it curved back toward the hallway. It contained a café table and two chairs and provided a modicum of privacy for two people to conduct their negotiations away from the crowd. Tanner nodded for her to sit, then opened the deck of cards.

"This is a new game to you," he told her, "so I would like you to make the first choices."

She took a deep breath, fanned out the cards, and started turning them over.

****

Tanner had to use every bit of his well-developed personal discipline to keep himself under control. His dick had hardened and swelled painfully the moment he set eyes on Kelly LeBlanc. And his entire body went on full alert. If he had less discipline, he'd have asked Reulas for a room right then, stripped her naked, and fucked her brains out.

What the hell?

The supple leather of her very short skirt barely covered the sweet curve of her ass. His hands itched to slide beneath the material and probe her cunt that the flimsy material shielded. Was she wet already? Did just the discussion of exhibitionism turn her on? The first time he'd participated in a demonstration, he was astounded at how the excitement of exhibitionism stimulated him. How intense his orgasm was when he finally gave up his self-control and allowed himself to experience it fully.

Twenty years ago, he had visited a dungeon near the base where he was training before he was selected for Delta Force. He'd gone with a friend, reluctantly, and become addicted after just one night. He'd learned the dungeons were a good place to put all that energy stored up from missions.

An experienced Dom had trained him, taught him to respect his subs, how to deal with bringing them out of subspace and reinforcing the importance of aftercare. In the clubs where he was a familiar figure, he was a sought-after Dom. He played right on the edge, but always with respect for his subs.

But with all the women he'd met, all the partners he'd had, none had ever been a punch to the gut like Kelly LeBlanc. He wanted to see her naked on her knees, hands behind her back, his cock in her mouth. Maybe with a plug in her butt and a vibrator keeping her right on the edge of orgasm. He might have a lot of self-control, but there was a hard edge to his desired methods of play. He hoped Kelly was ready for it, because after only one look, he certainly was. He shifted the fabric of his leather pants to ease the pressure on his swollen cock.

"Ready?" he prompted. If she licked her lip one more time, he was going to open his pants and thrust his cock into that tempting mouth.

She looked up at him. Whatever she saw in his eyes made her bow her head, cut the cards, and begin to lay them out.

He'd seen them all, of course. This was a game that worked for him whenever he was a guest at a new club or breaking in a new sub. It gave both parties a sense of what the other would tolerate, would want, would eventually crave.

He watched through narrowed eyes as she discarded some cards, placed others to the side. Interesting that she kept the picture of the St. Andrews Cross, the single tail whip, the electric violet wand, and the rider fucking ball. She paused at the three pictures of butt plugs, discarded two, and kept the medium sized one.

Oh, yeah. He wanted that plug in her ass while she rode the inflated ball with the dildo in her cunt. Blindfolded. Hands cuffed behind her back so her balance was unsteady. Shit!

He was getting hot just thinking about it. His cock hardened, his balls tingled, and the blood in his veins flowed in a heated rush. Her scent drifting up to his nostrils aroused him even more. He bet the juice of her pussy tasted like the finest nectar. Shit. His tongue tingled at the thought of it.

He watched as she shuffled through another few cards, kept the one with the paddle on it and the one with the spreader bar. When she hesitated at one, he leaned down to get a closer look.

Damn! One woman, two men, one with his cock in her ass, the other with his shaft in her mouth, with vibrating clothespins attached to her nipples. Reulas had been right about her. This woman was made for him. He'd looked for someone like her for a very long time. Good thing this was just for tonight.

If his instincts were right, he risked becoming addicted to her with more playtime. And that would be a huge mistake. Every sub he played with knew the rules from the beginning. No strings. One session or twenty, when he was through, it was over. No expectations. He had the uncomfortable feeling it wouldn't be that easy with Kelly LeBlanc.

He watched her go through the cards once again, setting the ones she preferred to avoid in one pile and those that she'd selected in another. She handed the rest of the deck to him.

"I hope my selections please you, Sir."

Oh, yeah. Damn straight.

But he went through the process of thumbing through them once more before nodding his head. He gave a quick glance through the ones she'd rejected, nodded again, then went through the rest of the cards.

There was little he rejected, but as much for show as anything he selected some of the harshest ones left and put them to the side. Then he handed her his choices. He forced himself to be patient as she looked them over one by one. Every muscle in his body tightened, and heat raced over his skin as he watched for her reaction.

Kelly silently studied the cards, eyes widening when she saw the drawing of the ball gag and the hood. She made no comment, just let out a slow breath and handed everything back to him.

"If there is anything I picked that you strongly object to," he said, "this is the time to tell me. Otherwise, I'll match up our choices and tell Reulas we're ready." Actually, he was more than ready.

"I'm fine with the selections…Master."

"I'll need to show Reulas the cards so he can make sure we have all the proper equipment. Once we're in the performance area, on the stage, he'll do the introductions."

Kelly rose with a fluid, graceful movement. Tanner headed back into the lounge area, very conscious of her behind him. He hoped, when the night was over, he could be satisfied with the pleasure and not want anything else. He just didn't do attachments. At all. Not anymore.

****

The performance area was to the right of the lounge, surrounded by a half-wall of glass so everyone had an unobstructed view. Kelly waited, head bowed, hands clasped behind her back, while Tanner had a long conversation with Reulas. It eased her unexpected anxiety that he took the time to check both their choices with the club owner. In the email, Reulas had said Tanner was a responsible Dom, but now, she saw for herself that the man was double-checking everything.

Then, he led her to the stage and placed her in the center, murmuring softly, "I will take good care of you, sub."

And even not knowing him, she believed him.

Battling a cross between nerves and anticipation, she stood on display for the crowd gathered behind the glass. Excitement shivered over her skin like little charges of electricity, her nipples tingled, and tiny spasms gripped the muscles in the walls of her cunt. Her pulse beat harder, and her breathing hitched.

Would he push her as close to the edge as she needed? Push her too close? No, she didn't think at this point in her sexual life there was such a thing as too close. Certainly not with this man, who pushed every sensual trigger in her body.

"Remove your clothes," he ordered. "Slowly, so the audience can enjoy each part of your body as you reveal it. But leave the boots on."

Kelly wasn't surprised. What was it with Doms and naked women and thigh high boots, anyway?

"Feet apart," he commanded. "Reulas is going to explain to the audience what we're doing."

Before she'd dressed tonight, in anticipation of what she would be asked to do, she'd rubbed lotion into every inch of her skin, including her freshly waxed pussy. A spotlight from the high ceiling bathed her in a golden halo. She deliberately took her time undressing, holding out each piece as she removed it, then letting it drop to the floor.

As she removed her clothes one item at a time, she spotted the flare of heat in Tanner's pale-gray eyes, a light he quickly banked, but it sent a thrill curling through her to know she'd put that heat there. Perhaps he wasn't as controlled and unaffected as he appeared.

A table containing a display of various toys and other items was wheeled across the stage as Reulas took his place in front of the stage, holding a wireless mic and the selections from the deck. As each item was used or each act performed, he would hold up the card for people to see.

"Tanner Sloat, a special guest tonight, has brought us a new game to introduce to the patrons of Rawhide." He held up the cards. "It's called Cut the Cards. Couples who opt to play this game will have a new deck of cards signed out to them. Each person goes through the deck, keeps the ones picturing the activities and positions they accept, discards the others, then the two compare their choices."

"Who makes the decision if one person chooses something the other person discarded?" one of the guests asked him.

"It's all negotiation," Reulas told him. "Just like every D/s relationship. Everything is negotiable for the comfort zone of both parties before the session begins. Tanner and I discussed this as a good way for Doms and subs who have never played together to learn each other's personal tastes. It's also a great way to spice up longstanding relationships.

"Kelly LeBlanc, a favorite of many of you, graciously accepted the invitation to perform with Tanner tonight. Right here on this stage, he will bring her to a tremendous climax for your visual enjoyment. As you can see, she is prepared and ready to play. So let the game begin."

She realized that Reulas had stopped speaking and Tanner was approaching her. He lifted two things from the table, and for a moment, she caught her breath. Then she forced herself to relax.

Whenever she'd accepted the use of the hood, soft leather that zipped behind her head, she'd had to battle a feeling of suffocation. But if she were to push herself out of her sexual comfort zone, a hood would have to be one of the things she accepted. So she'd left the card in their pile.

From the look in Tanner's eyes when he approached her, it appeared to be one of his favorite accessories. In his other hand, he held a ball gag by the straps that would hold the hood in place.

He stopped directly in front of her, his slate-gray

eyes boring into hers. "I need your safeword." His voice was low, rumbling through her like a wave of heat. The timbre of it made her pussy drip.

"Snakes."

His eyes widened a fraction. "Snakes?"

She dipped her head a fraction. "I hate snakes."

One corner of his mouth kicked up in a half-smile. "Then we'll have to be sure we don't expose you to any." He lifted the hood. "I'm going to put this on you now. I noticed your hesitation with the card. If you'd rather I not use this, here's your last chance to tell me."

Kelly couldn't say why, but she sensed she could trust this man completely. She'd had one very bad experience being hooded, and since then, just the idea edged her toward panic.

But although she had just met Tanner Sloat, he made her feel she could trust him implicitly. And an unexplained surge of desire to submit to him coaxed her to let him do whatever he wanted to her body.

"Put it on," she said at last. "I trust you."

He gave her a long look, then nodded. "Reulas said full sensory deprivation frightens you, so he selected a hood with openings for the eyes, the nostrils, and the mouth. It provides the feel of restriction, but still allows you to see and to breathe easily."

"Thank you, Sir," she whispered.

Her clit was already throbbing, even though neither the man nor any of the objects had touched it. Her cunt was so wet she could smell her own scent. Tanner's nostrils flared, an indication that he also caught it.

"Hands behind your back," he ordered.

With infinite gentleness, he tucked her hair behind her ears, then slid the hood carefully over her head. For one brief moment, she panicked.

He paused. "Just breathe, sub. If it's too much, say your safeword."

"I'm okay," she murmured, and suddenly she was.

He dipped his head in acknowledgment, settled the hood in place, and closed the zipper at the back. "Breathe."

She did, and the edge of anxiety was replaced by a craving for whatever he had in mind. Now she just wanted him to get on with it.

"Ball gag." He lifted it to show her. "Open your mouth."

The moment she did, he placed a round ball on her tongue. When she bit down on it, she was surprised to discover it was soft, made of a jellylike substance.

"I don't like the hard ones except in certain circumstances." He fastened the straps firmly at the back of her head. "This is our first time together, so I selected a hood that allows you to see and breathe, and a gag that will stifle your screams to a certain extent yet permit you to utter your safeword if necessary. I want you to trust me, sub."

She nodded to tell him she understood.

"Next card," Reulas said. "Manacles, so the sub is held firmly in place during the pleasure of the punishment."

An assistant lifted a large crosspiece from the table and screwed the base into the stage. Tanner guided Kelly's hands to the cuffs that dangled from the bar, securing them around her wrists.

"Spread your legs," he instructed.

When she did, he fastened cuffs around her ankles. She was now effectively restrained, legs spread wide, arms outstretched, unable to move in any direction. Her pulse galloped at the anticipation of what would come next.

"Butt plug." Through the openings in the hood, she saw Reulas display the card as he spoke. "Since she is a new sub with Tanner, we have chosen a medium-size plug for this evening." He looked to the right where the assistant waited. "Stage, please."

The man pressed a button in the wall, and the stage rotated so her back was to the audience. Now, she could no longer see Tanner, only her reflection in the glass wall. The image of her with the hood and the ball gag startled her, but it also stimulated her in a way she'd never expected. She was spread and manacled, exposed to everyone watching, and aroused beyond any expectations.

In the glass that enclosed the performance area, she caught the image of Tanner behind her, one hand smoothing over her ass, the strokes both calming and exciting. He trailed his fingers through the hot crease, up and down, finally pausing to press one fingertip against the puckered opening of her anus.

Focused on his reflection, she watched him move his head closer, close enough that she could hear him through the hood.

"I'm going to lube you up really good." He was close enough that she could feel his body heat against her back and her ass. He spoke just loud enough for her to hear him but not the audience. "When I cause you pain, it won't be this way."

She shivered with anticipation, dipping her head once to acknowledge his words.

When he pressed his fingers against her again, they

were coated with a cool gel, icy-hot against her sensitive opening. He stroked his wet fingers through the crease, around her opening, and finally slipped one finger into her rectum, rubbing her inner tissues. She gave a slight sound of protest when he withdrew his touch, but then he was back with more lube, this time using two fingers. And then a third, rubbing and stretching her to prepare her for the play. She was panting with need by the time the tip of the plug pushed against her opening.

Tanner separated her cheeks with one strong hand while, with the other, he slowly pushed the plug inside. Its surface was pebbled, each little bump like an electric stimulation.

"Breathe," he reminded her. "In and out."

And then it was fully seated, filling her completely. She clenched the cheeks of her buttocks around it, but with her legs spread apart, it was hard to get any pressure. Tremors raced through the walls of her cunt and spread throughout her body. He had barely done anything to her, and she was already trembling with need.

Vaguely, she heard Reulas telling the crowd something else, but she was already so stimulated she couldn't pay attention to him. She just waited for the next stage in the performance. Whip? Paddle? Vibrator? The idea of any of them ramped up a need already spiraling out of control.

What was it about tonight? She'd been through this before, a performance for the members and guests. Okay, the hood was new, but the restraints were not. Or the plug. Or anything else in the cards. So what was the extra factor here? It had to be the man himself. Tanner

Sloat radiated so much masculine appeal, so much sex, that she'd been on the verge of climax from the moment Reulas introduced them.

Relax. Breathe. Think of something else.

But it was damn hard when, from the first moment she'd seen him, she'd been willing to do almost anything he asked of her. Almost.

She closed her eyes, reaching for some measure of control. A good sub didn't give in to her body's demands until her Master gave her permission. She wasn't about to embarrass either Reulas or Tanner—or herself—by letting an unbidden climax roll through her. She drew in a deep breath, let it out, and focused on what was happening.

Her eyes flew open, however, at the touch of Tanner's fingers on her pussy. He stroked the length of her slit, up and down, before giving her clit a pinch. She gasped and tried to rock into his hand, but he moved it away. A motor hummed, and the stage revolved again so she faced the audience.

"I had no idea how tempting and delicious you'd be," he said in a low voice. "I think we'll finish the first half of the performance here and then take it to someplace more private."

Her eyes widened. The ball gag prevented her from saying anything, but her mind whirled with ideas. Had she disappointed him in some way? There were cards both of them had pulled that involved his cock in her mouth. A dildo in her pussy while he sucked her clit. His shaft between her breasts, rubbing until he climaxed and shot his cum all over them. Why weren't they going to do those things?

But it wasn't her place to ask. Besides, she could

barely focus on what was happening now. Especially when Tanner's fingers were replaced by the touch of metal, the pinch of a clit vibrator, and thin spirals of electricity shocked through her body. She was glad for the manacles, because they were the only things stabilizing her trembling body.

Watching through the openings in the hood, she saw Tanner stop in front of the table, study its contents, and then pick up the single tail whip. If he had selected the paddle, she would have accepted it. Her choice, after all. But with all the other sensations pummeling her body, she wasn't sure she'd have been able to handle the flat *thwack* of the hard wood.

Yes, you can. You can handle anything.

Not with her senses as amped up as they were right now. She was sure if Tanner touched her again with his hand, she'd implode right there in front of everyone. And that would be such a violation.

He stretched out the length of the single tail and ran it over her body, shoulders to thighs, breast to breast. Along the inside of her thighs while the little clit vibrator hummed busily and her body shivered in response.

He strolled lazily around her, drawing the tail of the whip across one palm. She sensed when he stopped and tried to prepare herself for what would come next. When the tip of the lash struck her buttocks, she flinched slightly and bit down on the ball gag. The next strike came immediately, then the next and the next. Her ass, her back, the backs of her thighs. She ground her teeth so hard into the ball gag she wondered if she'd bite clear through it. Tears ran down her cheeks. Her body was so ready for orgasm it took every ounce of control she could dredge up not to let it roll over her.

She waited for the next strike of the whip, but instead, Tanner's hand smoothed over the skin on her back, curving over her ass. Then his head was close to hers so she could hear him through the hood.

"I'm going to let you come now, but don't make a sound." His low voice rumbled through her.

She nodded.

In the next moment, he slid a dildo into her pussy, filling her completely, increasing the pressure from the butt plug. He turned it on, and the instant the pulsations shimmied through her she exploded. The walls of her cunt gripped the vibrator, clamping down on it. The muscles of her ass clenched. She dug her nails into the palms of her hands, every bit of her body shaking as if tossed by a violent wind. It went on and on until she wasn't sure if she could take it for one more moment. If she hadn't had the ball gag, she was sure she would have bitten through her tongue.

Then Tanner was there, rubbing her back again, her arms, her ass as the last of the aftershocks finally rippled through her. Limp, spent, she waited weakly for whatever came next. She barely heard the sounds of the applause or Reulas' concluding remarks. Wordless, Tanner removed the clit vibrator and slid both the dildo and butt plug from her body. He released the manacles from her wrists and her ankles and lifted her in his arms.

"Show's over for tonight," he murmured against the hood. "Let's get you to some place more private."

****

Kelly closed her eyes, wondering if he was just going to leave the hood and gag in place. At the moment, she was so weak and spent she almost didn't care. Almost.

She leaned into Tanner's chest as he carried her out of the performance area. He stopped for a moment, then moved forward again. She heard the soft click of a door opening and closing. In another moment, he deposited her on a soft padded surface, sitting her upright, bracing her with one arm.

She leaned into him as he unfastened the ball gag and eased it from her mouth. Then, he unzipped the hood and slipped it over her head, tossing it to the side. She blinked her eyes, focusing and realizing she was seated on a thickly padded bench in one of the private rooms.

"I'm a mess," she mumbled.

"We'll fix that. Not to worry." His voice was soft and soothing, such a contrast to the uncompromising hardness of his appearance.

Moving her head so it rested against his shoulder, he pulled wet wipes from a bowl next to her and carefully cleaned her face. She was embarrassed to realize her nose had been running, the mucous mixing with her tears.

"It's okay," he soothed. "You did very well, sub. Reulas said you were the perfect one for this, and he was right. Whoever trained you did it well."

Kelly's mind took a brief trip back in time, remembering the Dom who had taught her so well, taking her from that first discovery of who and what she was to the point where she became one of the most sought after subs at whatever club she visited.

"I had planned to use the violet wand before the single tail whip," he told her. "The low voltage electricity it emits ramps up the effect of both vibrators I used. But you're so damn responsive, I was afraid I'd push you over the edge too soon, no matter how you tried to hold on."

"Thank you."

He brushed her hair back from her face. "My pleasure."

Lifting her from the table, he carried her to a large armchair in one corner, pausing on the way to pull a bottle of water from the minifridge and grab a quilt from the rack where it was stored. In a moment, he had them both in the chair. With great tenderness, he wrapped the quilt around her and settled her on his lap.

"Drink," he ordered, uncapping the bottle and holding it to her lips.

They sat like that for a long time, her muscles easing, the water rehydrating her body, Tanner stroking her hair, her back, her shoulders. He never said a word, so she didn't, either.

But finally, she had to ask him the question poking at the back of her brain. "Why didn't you use the rest of the cards? I accepted them with no problem."

He cupped her chin and turned her head so she faced him. "Don't repeat this to anyone." A corner of his mouth almost kicked up in a hint of a smile. "But it stopped being just a performance to me halfway through it."

She frowned. "I don't understand."

"I'm not sure I do, either." He looked away, staring across the room at the wall. "One of the important things you learn in Delta Force is having complete control of yourself. The missions we get sent on require it. Otherwise, we could get ourselves and our team

21

members killed. For me, the only way to do that was to lock away my emotions completely."

"That must have been very difficult to do."

He shrugged. "Not so much, but it meant relationships were a no-go. Being able to come to different dungeons around the world to play has been a great stress reliever."

"I sense a 'but' in there," she prompted.

"But tonight, when Reulas introduced us, something hit me like an exploding IED. I never believed in instant chemistry before, but Jesus, Kelly. I looked at you, and you nearly took me down to my knees."

She burrowed into his chest, unwilling to look at him while she made her own confession. "I, um, had the same reaction. Rawhide is like a second home to me. I can play without worrying about messy relationships. Maybe because no one ever aroused my emotions the way you did. Do," she amended.

Tanner's body tensed. He was silent for so long she was afraid she'd made a misstep here. Did he just plan to tell her how he felt and move on?

"Listen," she said, "if you—"

He touched a finger to her lips. "Shh. It's okay. It's just a shock to me to have someone say that to me. I've made sure to let every woman I've ever been with know the score. It's all about the physical. The sex. Nothing more."

"And this?" she prompted.

"I don't know, Kelly. It's so foreign to me. I know that right now I'm hard as a spike. I want to fuck you but not with toys or anything. Just you and me, my cock in your pussy. But I know you must be sore and wrung out."

She brushed her fingers along his cheek. "Not too sore for that. If that's all we do."

He studied her face. "Are you sure?"

"I am." At least she hoped she was. Already, her body was responding to him, and he'd barely touched her at all.

"I want to kiss you. Kissing's always a fantasy to me, too, because it's so personal."

She shifted in his lap, brought his head down to hers, and pressed her mouth to his. His lips were firm and warm, and when she opened hers, his tongue swept inside, a living flame heating her flesh. He drank from her as she did from him, tongues tangling in an erotic dance. Unbelievably, her pussy was getting wet again, her core rocketing to life with need.

He tore his mouth from hers, trailing his tongue along the line of her jaw and nibbling the lobe of her ear with his teeth. He threaded his fingers through her hair, holding her in place while he kissed his way down her throat, to the hollow where her pulse beat, to the upper swell of her breasts just visible in the gap of the quilt.

"If you're absolutely sure," he said again, "let's ditch this quilt."

Kelly shrugged out of it, trying not to wince as certain muscles protested.

"Stop." Tanner stilled her hands. "You're hurting. This won't work."

She smiled. "I'm fine. I promise I wouldn't lie to you. Okay?"

****

Tanner wanted so badly to believe Kelly. He was

still struggling with the force of the impact she had on him, with the stewpot she'd made out of his emotions. But damn! He wanted to get his cock inside her in the worst way.

One thing about Reulas. He had every one of his private rooms set up so no matter where one wanted to fuck or play, whatever one needed was right at hand. Securing Kelly with one arm, he pushed the lever that turned the chair into a lounger. Then, he reached into the drawer of the little table beside it to pull out a handful of condoms.

"Aren't you optimistic." She laughed.

"One can hope. Anyway, we have the room for as long as we want it. But if we only fuck once, I'll die a happy man."

"I think I can take care of that for you with no problem."

Sliding to her knees, she unzipped his fly and freed his thick, swollen cock, holding it in both hands while she took a long look at it. Then she slowly lowered her head and took the thick breadth of him into her mouth. Strange. Here they were in a club with every instrument of pleasure imaginable, every opportunity for the kinkiest of sex, and the thing that seemed to be turning them both on right now was straight, vanilla sex. How funny was that?

Then she closed her lips around him and sucked hard, squeezing his abundant length with her tongue, and every thought flew out of his head.

"Shit, Kelly." He slid his fingers through her hair to hold her head in place. "You have the sweetest mouth this side of heaven. Suck me hard, baby. Real hard."

She did just that. Sliding one hand between his thighs, she cupped the sac holding his balls and gently squeezed. Heat jolted through him. He groaned and tightened his grip on her head. He wasn't going to last like this, as much as he loved it.

Roughly, he pulled her head away.

She looked up at him, frowning. "What's wrong?"

He gave a ragged laugh. "What's wrong is I'm about ten seconds away from the top of my head blowing off. Straddle me, sub, so I can see if that sweet pussy is still wet enough for me."

He helped her to rise and positioned her so her thighs bracketed his. He slid one hand between her thighs to her cunt and smiled when he found it still dripping. Damn.

He just might have found the woman of his dreams. Then he had to stop thinking because he was so close to the edge he was ready to topple over. Sheathing himself with one of the condoms, he lifted her and brought her down right on his dick.

He closed his eyes at the intense sensations that raced through him when her snug pussy closed around him, grasping it with her wet heat. Holy shit! He gritted his teeth, reaching for whatever control he had. The performance had him so ramped up anyway he hoped he lasted long enough to give Kelly one more orgasm.

The image of her naked body, butt plug and vibrators in place, back and ass crisscrossed with beautiful red stripes from the whip was a jolt to his system. He had to do something to move this along because his famous discipline had gone to shit.

He slipped one hand between them, found her already sore and swollen clit, and rubbed it with his thumb. Again and again, pinching and stroking while her inner muscles gripped him and her breathing quickened. Her hot liquid drenched him with a sudden rush.

"I'm ready." Her voice was breathy and strained.

"Yes, you are, darlin'." Gripping her hips, he lifted her up and brought her down again. "Ride me, now."

She balanced her hands on his shoulders and rocked back and forth and up and down. The slide of her pussy against his cock was like the glide of smooth silk. Up and down, again and again. And somehow, as if their bodies were completely in tune, they arrived at the orgasm together and crashed into rocket-filled space.

Long minutes passed while they rode out the shattering spasms. He wrapped his arms around her, holding her tightly against him. Her breasts pressed into his chest, her nipples like hot, hard points. Her cunt milked him over and over as he spurted into the latex.

And then it was done. She collapsed against him, her breathing as raspy as his. He held her tightly, smoothing the damp hair from her forehead, brushing light kisses on her damp skin. Kisses? He didn't kiss. Jesus, he really had fallen into an alternate universe. But hadn't he known that from the moment he laid eyes on her?

He finally lifted her from him so he could dispose of the condom, easing himself slowly from her silken grasp. When he returned to the chair and settled her in his lap again, he held the cards they hadn't used that night.

She looked at them and then at him, a smile curving her lips, swollen from sucking his cock. "I hate to tell you this, but I don't think I'm up to the rest of the deal tonight."

He chuffed a laugh. "Darlin', neither am I. And I never thought I'd say that." He adjusted her in his lap so they could look at the cards together. "But tomorrow night? Now that's another story."

She gave a breathy chuckle. "So just to be sure. You want to meet me back here tomorrow night? For another performance?"

"Hell, no." When her body tightened, he brushed a kiss on her cheek. A kiss! Shit! He really was falling hard. "This is going to be completely private." He turned over the first card. "St. Andrew's Cross and the paddle." The next card. "Me fucking you in the ass." And the next one. "Wax play. I could draw some really erotic designs on that luscious body of yours. And I'd sure like to feel my cock in your mouth again, maybe with a dildo in that pretty little pussy, making you want to come but you won't until I do. Until you suck me off good."

"You think we'll get to all that in one night? I don't know if I'll survive."

"Well, see, that's the nice thing about this place. Reulas has given me a guest pass with no expiration. We might even try a second deck of cards." He gave her a serious look. "Think you can handle that? Reulas says you usually only play one night on the weekend."

"I think, for you, I might make an exception."

"Good. That's good." He tilted her face up to his. "You have anything you need to get home for? Pets that have to be fed? Family members looking for you?"

She shook her head. "No pets. And all my family lives in other places."

"Okay, then. I've got a nice suite with a great spa tub at that new hotel downtown. Right now, I'd like to take you there and spend the rest of the night and tomorrow pampering the hell out of you." He stroked her cheek. "Get you in shape for tomorrow night."

She looked at him hard, questions in her eyes. "Tanner, how did this happen? We came in here two independent individuals, and something just exploded between us."

"Shocked the shit out of me, too. But you know what? Maybe it's an unexpected gift, and we should try to appreciate it."

She grinned. "As long as it comes with a new deck of cards."

He brushed his mouth over hers. "I guess anything can happen in Rawhide."

Blackjack

"I'm glad you arranged this for me, Kelly." Nia March inched forward on the back seat of the car. "Thanks so much."

"And I'm just glad you agreed to come with us." Kelly LeBlanc turned her head and grinned at her friend as they turned into the parking lot for Rawhide. "You'll enjoy the club."

"And Blackjack." Tanner Sloat's deep voice rumbled from the driver's seat.

Yes, Blackjack, the Dom Tanner had arranged for her to meet tonight, along with her first introduction to the new card game at Rawhide. The game that had brought Kelly and Tanner together. A little shiver of anticipation raced over Nia's skin.

Kelly shifted in the front seat, turning as much as her seat belt would allow. "It seems so long since we've done this together."

"Because five years ago you moved from Dallas to San Antonio," Nia pointed out.

"To take a fabulous job," Kelly reminded her.

"I know, I know. But I miss going clubbing with you."

"And that's why you came for a visit. And you got to meet the fabulous Tanner Sloat." Kelly touched the thin gold collar that circled her neck. "Master of all Masters."

"And don't you forget it," Tanner chuckled, pulling smoothly into a parking place.

"As if."

Nia tamped down the tiny bit of jealousy that surged up at their intense connection. Even in the tenor of their voices, an almost tangible physical desire arced between them.

Kelly had searched for a long time for just the right Dom. She'd had so many disappointments, and Nia held her hand through them all. It thrilled her to see her friend so happy, but she couldn't help wondering if she would ever find that for herself. That one person with whom she had an instant link. Someone who lit sparks in her body and aroused her just by looking in her direction. She'd seen the instant spark in others. Kelly had told her that was how it had been with Tanner. But to Nia, it seemed as if she'd been seeking that dream forever.

She forced away the negative thoughts. "I'm thrilled for you. You know that."

"I do. And maybe tonight you'll find the Master of *your* dreams," Kelly teased.

"Maybe. Possibly. And if not, no biggie." She unbuckled her seat belt. "I'm excited just thinking about this card game."

"What could be more appropriate for a sub whose scene name is Queen of Hearts, right?"

"Right." She did think it was an incredible coincidence. "And who's getting ready to play Cut the Cards with a hot Dom."

"You know he's hot?" Nia grinned.

"Have you met him?"

"No, but Tanner's recommendation is good enough

for me. He knows not to put you with just anyone."

"Damn straight," Tanner told her. "Kelly would hand me my ass if I did, and I might be the one getting to feel the whip."

"So…" Kelly half-turned in her seat. "You ready?"

"I am. Let's go."

They climbed out of the car, and she waited while Tanner locked it.

"Let's move," he said.

"You'll love it." Kelly winked and linked her arm though Nia's.

Tanner pushed the button set into the frame of the heavy carved front door. It swung outward, and Nia followed him and Kelly inside. The vestibule was circular in shape, large enough for a stand to hold a guest book and a small bench, with a hallway leading to the rest of the club. Nia stood behind her friend while Tanner checked them into the club with the doorman who had recently been hired.

"Good evening, Anton. We made arrangements with Reulas for our guest, Nia March, Queen of Hearts."

The doorman nodded and checked their names off in the open book on the stand. "Yes, it's right here." He looked at Nia. "I'll need to see your membership card from your home club."

Nia slid it out of the little pocket in the leather miniskirt she wore and handed it to him. She waited while he scanned it and handed it back.

"Enjoy yourselves this evening."

"Thank you." Tanner led the way down the little hallway, Kelly and Nia following appropriately behind him.

When they moved into the main area, Nia saw that it was divided into two sections—a lounge and a performance area. The lounge was almost completely occupied, most of the tables, couches, and armchairs filled with people talking in soft tones. Some of the subs sat on the floor at the feet of their Masters. A couple had leashes attached to their collars.

Nia noticed one Dom in particular who had most of the leash wrapped around his free hand, keeping his sub's upper body close to his crotch. His other hand held a drink that he sipped on while his sub stroked his exposed cock.

Two men sat side by side on a couch, conversing quietly. A woman lay across both their laps, eyes closed while one man fondled her breasts and the other played with her pussy beneath her skirt. Nia wondered idly if she belonged to both or if her Dom was just in a sharing mood tonight.

Tanner obviously had perks in the place, because he commandeered a love seat against one wall, the occupants simply smiling as they moved away without question.

"Sit," he ordered the two women. "Hands folded. Legs apart." He looked at Nia, and a tiny smile hitched up one corner of his mouth. "For the moment, consider me your temporary Dom." He leaned down and winked. "I'd hate for anyone to think I'd brought a sub who didn't obey orders."

Nia swallowed a grin, moved her knees apart, and folded her hands demurely in her lap.

"Very good. I need to speak to Reulas. In the meantime, I'll have someone bring you cold drinks."

Nia knew that, like many well-run private

dungeons, Rawhide did not serve alcoholic beverages. Kelly had explained that, at one time, they had discussed permitting people to drink if they weren't going to play, but then vetoed it because people could change their minds.

Reulas, the Dungeon Master, had a hard and fast rule about alcohol. He wanted his members and guests to be aware at all times of their choices. But Nia didn't mind. The club she and Kelly had belonged to in Dallas—the one in which she was still a member—had the same rule.

She wondered where the Dom who Tanner had told her about was and how soon she'd get to meet the man he'd arranged for her to play with tonight.

"You can trust Tanner's judgment," Kelly teased. "Really. He wouldn't set you up with a Dom who would turn you off."

A pair of legs clad in gray slacks came into her field of vision, and she looked up to see a waiter holding a tray with two glasses.

"Master Tanner ordered sparkling water for you." He dipped his head then placed a glass in her hand and in Kelly's. "I'm sure Master Tanner will let me know if you need a refill."

Nia sipped at her drink, letting the bubbles explode on her tongue, mingling with the bubbles of excitement fizzing through her bloodstream. She was playing a game with herself, trying to imagine what the mysterious stranger looked like, when, in her peripheral vision, she caught people moving their way. She recognized Tanner's boots right away.

"Time for introductions," Tanner said. "You may look up. Both of you."

Nia lifted her gaze, and her breath caught in her throat. Every nerve in her body snapped, and her heart actually stuttered. Good lord! This man was a lethal weapon even before he uttered a word. Something deep inside began to unfold and excitement jittered through her nerve endings.

The man's presence filled the space between them. His hair was the color of ebony, short and expensively layered. Thick, black lashes emphasized his all-seeing eyes, lashes that were the envy of every woman who saw them. She wondered if there was some kind of machine or whatever that created Doms like this to satisfy the hungry needs of subs. The thought almost made her giggle, but she bit her tongue, unwilling to embarrass herself.

The outline of a mouthwateringly thick cock pressed against the soft fabric of his pants, and her mouth suddenly went dry as she imagined the feel of it on her tongue, in her pussy, or even her ass. She could almost smell the scent of her arousal. She knew in her bones that whatever this man wanted from her she'd be more than willing to give, with no restraint or holding back.

"Queen of Hearts, meet Blackjack." Tanner's voice held a touch of humor.

"The man himself? Master of the card game?" Her lips twitched as she tried to suppress a smile.

"Queen of Hearts. How appropriate." The voice was rich and deep, a little like Tanner's but thicker and with a Texas twang that made every nerve ending fire up. "Stand up, sub. Let me take a look at all of you."

Oh, yes. His voice might have that Texas warmth, but there was no mistaking the tone of command or the strength in his words. Nia rose on slightly shaky legs, clasped her hands in front of her, and bowed her head.

"You may keep your head raised, sub. I want to get a good look at your face."

She could almost feel the power of his gaze as it traveled over her body. Now she understood the saying, "He ate her up with his eyes," because she sensed it as they devoured her. She felt completely naked, every stitch of clothing gone, every part of her body exposed to him.

While she stood there, trying not to shiver beneath his scrutiny, another man strolled up, shook hands with Tanner.

He nodded to Blackjack, holding out his hand. "Welcome to Rawhide, Blackjack. I'm Clint Chavez, one of the owners. You come highly recommended from your home club."

Blackjack chuckled. "Yes. I've been a member there for a long time. Thanks for the guest pass."

"Our pleasure." Clint pulled a sealed deck of cards from his pocket along with a key card and handed them both to Blackjack. "Tanner explained that you requested a private room. Number three, down the hall on the left." He flicked his gaze over Nia before looking at Blackjack again. "Enjoy your evening."

Blackjack turned to Tanner. "I'll see you later?"

Tanner nodded. "Just text me when the Queen of Hearts is ready for her ride home." He looked at Kelly and grinned. "We'll be playing our own card game."

Blackjack tapped Nia on the shoulder. "Time to go."

With a last glance at Kelly, Nia followed the man out of the lounge and down the hallway. She waited obediently while he inserted the key card and opened the door to the room, then followed him inside.

As soon as the lock clicked on the door, he turned to face her. "Safeword. Now. I never begin without it."

Nia wet her lips and swallowed. "Scarlet."

He cocked one eyebrow. "Scarlet?"

She nodded. "It's the color of the queen's gown. The Queen of Hearts represents womanhood. That's why I chose the name."

A combination of heat and approval swirled in his eyes. "Excellent. As long as it wasn't from that foulmouthed woman in the fairy tale."

"No." She wet her lips again. "Sir."

"Scarlet it is." He studied her. "We don't know anything about each other except that our friends have put us together. I have to ask you, do you trust me? After just a few minutes together?"

At once, she realized there was much more to him than just the cravings of the lifestyle. This was a man who knew what a D/s relationship was all about, who probably would live it with the right sub. Who had substance and wanted the relationship to be meaningful whether it was for an hour or twenty-four/seven.

"I— They said I would be safe with you. I trust them, so yes, I trust you."

"Excellent." His eyes mesmerized her until she couldn't—wouldn't—look away. "Then we begin."

Her gaze tracked him as he walked to the center of the room, motioning for her to follow him. "Before I open the deck of cards, I want you to remove all of your clothing." His gaze flicked to her feet. "Except for those shoes."

"Yes, Master."

"I always like to lay everything out for my subs the first time we play together. To begin with, I prefer Sir rather than Master as the honorific."

"Sir," she repeated. "Yes, Sir."

He focused his eyes intently on her face. "Is that insolence, sub?"

"No, Sir." She bit her lower lip. "Well, perhaps a little," she teased. Damn! Kelly had always told her that streak of impudence would get her in trouble.

"If it is, you know you will need to be severely punished."

Oh, yes. Please.

"Or perhaps that is the goal. We'll see." He paused. "Next thing. I expect absolute obedience from my sub at all times. No matter what we are doing. Is that clear? If it is, nod your head."

After she did so, he dropped lithely into an armchair set to the side, rested one ankle on the opposite knee, and tore open the wrapping on the cards. But his eyes never left her.

They had barely had a conversation. He hadn't asked her any questions except for her safeword, although she was sure Tanner had filled him in on her history and sexual desires. But she felt connected to him in some mystical way, as if they'd known each other forever and they were only playing at being strangers. Odd, because she'd never had that feeling with any Dom before, even the ones she talked with at length before their first session together.

Kelly had told her with a secret smile that was the way it had been with her and Tanner. Was lightning about to strike twice in the same club?

Slowly, she unbuttoned her short cutaway vest,

opened it, and let it slide down her arms to the floor. She had chosen to forego a bra, so she was left naked from the waist up.

The moment his eyes focused on her breasts, her nipples hardened into painful points and her breasts ached with need. She swallowed and slid down the side zipper on the skirt that barely covered her pussy. A flick of her wrist and it joined her vest on the floor. That left her in the sexy sandals and the tiniest red thong.

When she hooked her thumbs in the elastic at the sides, he held up his hand. "Come closer. I want to do that."

He placed both feet on the floor, legs apart and motioned for Nia to stand between them. As soon as she did, he ran his hands lazily over her body, palming her breasts, then pinching her nipples. Soft at first, then harder and harder until he noticed her first flinch of pain.

"Sensitive nipples. Excellent. I have just the thing for them."

She knew he expected silence, so she stood mutely as he continued to follow the dips and contours of her flesh, sketching her with his fingers. When he came to the thong, he tugged it until the elastic rested low at her hips, then ran his fingers down the hot crease between the globes of her ass. Unexpectedly, he pinched each rounded cheek, hard, as he'd done with her nipples. Moisture flooded her cunt and trickled to the inside of her thighs.

Lust burned in Blackjack's eyes at her response. "Are you a pain junkie, Queen of Hearts? Does pain turn you on?"

She nodded, once.

"Good. I understand there are some interesting cards in this deck relating to methods of pain."

He continued to draw the thong down her legs until it reached her ankles. His gaze took in every inch of her pussy, naked except for a carefully trimmed line of curls on each lip. He carefully stroked one finger down each row, then dipped his finger into her slit. When he removed it, he brought it to his mouth and licked it very slowly.

Her entire body clenched at the sight. Heat surged through her, warming her pussy even more and sending tiny electrical charges to her nipples.

"You're a delicious treat. I expect to taste a lot more of you before the evening is over. You may discard the thong now."

Balancing so she didn't tumble off her high heels, she stepped out of the miniscule piece of lingerie and kicked it to the side.

Blackjack removed the cards from their box, riffled them twice, then shuffled them.

"Time to set the game, sub. Some people like to go through the deck one time and remove all the cards representing things totally unacceptable. Then each person gets to select from what's left. The way I prefer is to each make our selections first time around and discard the rest."

She wet her lips again. "Whatever pleases you, Sir."

"Good. I will allow you to make the first selections." He pulled over a small table next to the chair and set the cards on it. "Cut them. Then I'll deal. But choose wisely."

After she separated the pile at almost exactly the halfway mark, he began turning over the cards one at a time. The third card was a woman on her knees, hands cuffed behind her, feet spread wide with a stretcher bar. A man stood beside her applying a flogger with rubber tips. A surge of desire coursed through her at the memory of the exquisite pain those tips created.

"That one." She nodded.

Blackjack set the card aside, then continued turning them over. When he came to one with a woman stretched on a St. Andrews Cross, face up, weights attached to her nipples and clit, and a man applying an electric wand, she pointed again. And again he set it aside.

By the time they'd gone through the deck, she'd also chosen one with the single tail whip, a short but wide paddle, and a stainless-steel butt plug with a place to include liquid that would give the tissues a pleasant burn.

"Interesting choices," he commented. "All right. My turn."

She studied each of the cards he selected and set on top of her choices—a woman on a spanking bench; a woman stretched out by a wall, arms upraised, legs wide apart, manacles on ankles and wrists, a large plug in her butt, and the edge of a vibrator extending from her cunt; a woman on her knees, hands cuffed behind her while she wrapped her lips around her Master's cock.

"Only three?" she asked, then realized she'd spoken without permission.

A slow grin spread over Blackjack's face. "Impudence again. I think we need to attend to that."

He picked up the card depicting the rubber-tipped flogger. "We'll begin with this."

Nia's pussy was dripping and throbbed with need, and she eagerly anticipated the rush of endorphins the pain would release in her body. She could hardly wait to begin.

****

For the first time in a long time, Jack "Blackjack" Blackwell was having a problem keeping his shit together.

The plan had been simple. Pop into San Antonio for a few days on business, hook up with his old friend Tanner Sloat, score a guest pass at whatever club Tanner now belonged to, and spend a couple of nights satisfying his urges as a Dom. All he was looking for was a chance to play with someone new before he headed back to Dallas. To relieve the tension of countless long days of grueling business meetings.

He'd been shocked the first time he realized how much he enjoyed the kinky side of sex. Administering pain, seeing a sub enjoy the effects of it. The rush of pheromones through her system and the physical effects were unignorable across her flesh. The adrenaline rush, for her as she embraced the pain and for himself as he administered and knew it was giving her pleasure. Having someone trust him enough to put herself completely under his control. Knowing he had that power—a power he'd never abused—always gave him a rush.

He enjoyed being unattached, spending his playtime at the club where he was a member. The few times he'd tried to form a relationship, it had sputtered and died. He'd begun to wonder if he just wasn't cut out for anything permanent. Would he want to live the lifestyle twenty-four/seven? Only at home? In the clubs? He'd seen other couples embrace it, but somehow, he'd always had the feeling he'd lose who he was if he committed to only one person.

When Tanner had told him about Rawhide and their new shtick, a Cut the Cards game, he was intrigued. What a great way for both a Dom and his sub to find out right from the start what their preferences were and be able to get right to it. Tanner and his sub, Kelly—who his friend recently collared—had a friend visiting who they planned to bring to the club with them. Someone they thought he'd enjoy.

Enjoy? He didn't know if he wanted to get tangled up in that. What if it turned out badly? If the session were a disaster in some way, wouldn't it endanger his friendship with Tanner? But then they'd introduced him to the Queen of Hearts, and every part of his body went on high alert.

Holy shit!

The minute he laid eyes on her something inside him had flared to life, something totally unexpected. Something he wasn't sure he was ready to deal with at this point in his life. That elusive something—a combination of the physical and emotional—zipped around him like an electrical field. And that was before they'd even entered the private room.

Now, as he sat in his chair and looked at her, he wondered if the hand of fate he'd always made fun of had finally touched him, if the magic that Tanner had found with Kelly was whispering over him.

When he looked at the cards she'd chosen, all of them representing intense pain in one form or another, something sizzled in his blood. If tonight turned out the way he thought it might, he was in such trouble. This was just supposed to be a one-nighter. He didn't even know where she lived or how he'd see her again.

First things first.

"I don't expect we'll get through all of these." He'd be exhausted if they did. He picked up the card depicting the rubber-tipped flogger. "I think we'll start here. On your knees, sub, facing away from me. Hands behind your back."

When she dropped into position, his cock swelled and pressed against the fabric of his slacks, and an ache gripped his balls. Slowly, he walked to the cabinet on the wall, opened it, and selected the things he needed.

When he knelt beside her to fasten the handcuffs, he stroked his hand over her again, her smooth skin carrying the scent of fresh flowers and teasing at his senses. He was silent while he clicked the cuffs into place, and when he pushed her legs apart so he could fasten the manacles on the spreader bar around her ankles.

She tottered a little, off-balance because of the position. He threaded his fingers through the silk of her hair and guided her head down so her forehead touched the floor. She'd be better stabilized this way but also more vulnerable. He loved that vulnerability, and it struck him that he enjoyed it even more with this woman he barely knew than any of his other previous playmates.

He was about to be in big trouble.

Without any warning, he struck her ass cheek with the flat of his hand, low on the curve. She jerked slightly, but the sound she made was a moan of pleasure. His cock flexed in response.

Sliding his fingers down through the hot crevice, he reached her pussy and thrust two fingers inside. Jesus! She was soaked. When he slid his fingers out, he rubbed them along the length of her slit, pinching her clit from behind.

With other subs, there was always an understanding. He gave them what they craved, and they did the same for him. A fair exchange. But with his Queen, he felt a build-up of connectedness, a bonding that grew stronger in just a few moments. As her trust became more and more evident, the strength of the power exchange grew deeper.

This was more than he'd ever felt, even with subs he played with frequently. When he finally fucked her tonight, finally let himself have his own release, he had a feeling his entire life would be on the verge of change.

Picking up the instrument with the hard rubber tips, he delivered another smack to her buttocks, and another, enjoying both the manner in which the red of the heat spread across her skin and the little cries of pleasure that puffed from her mouth.

She made no attempt to move away from the contact. Rather, she somehow adjusted her body in its awkward position so her ass was higher, more accessible. He had to restrain himself from bending down and licking the hot flesh.

The hard rubber tips did their job, stinging the flesh where they landed. His Queen cried out and tried to squeeze her thighs together, but the spreader bar prevented it.

Blackjack was good at this, at knowing just how to space the blows, how hard to swing the instrument, how many blows to deliver. Again, he struck her ass, then her thighs, then back to her ass. He teased himself as well as her by pausing every two or three strikes to slide his hand over her reddened skin and his fingers into her cunt. He hadn't thought it possible for her to get any wetter, but by now she was dripping. Her walls clutched at him, vibrating against his touch.

"Do you want to come, sub?"

She drew in a long breath, nodded her head, and whispered, "Yes."

"Yes, what?"

"Yes, I want to come, Sir."

He cupped her pussy with his palm. "Not yet. We've hardly begun." He pinched her clit and was rewarded with another of those little pleasurable sounds.

He still struggled to understand why he was trying to make more of this than just the one night. When he hooked up with subs in his home club, they enjoyed each other for the time they were together, and the only thing he worried about was making sure his sub was as satisfied as he was at the end of the session. But with this woman, he felt a difference, had from the first moment he saw her. He was gripped with an overwhelming need to excel, to make this special.

Backing away from her, he unzipped his fly and took a moment to squeeze his cock, trying to appease its demands. It wouldn't do for his release to explode before he was ready.

Then, tucking his shaft back into his slacks, he knelt beside his Queen, running his hand over the smooth surface of her skin from her spine to her glowing buttocks to her reddened thighs. She trembled beneath his touch, her breathing still choppy and escalated after the spanking and the flogger. He released the catches on the spreader and pushed it away, so tempted to just kneel behind her and plunge deep, fucking her like some stallion in heat. His famous self-control was fast eroding, shredded by the unexpected impact of this woman. He wasn't even sure he would survive this evening.

Get your act together.

He removed the handcuffs and rubbed the muscles of her arms to ease the strain. What next? If he wasn't going to last a lot longer, what card would he choose? He rested his hand on the slope of her buttocks while she quivered beneath his touch. He was amazed and pleased at how completely she embraced the pain.

Okay, make this good, jackass. Make it good for her, and maybe, just maybe, she'll see you again. If she's in town any longer.

He helped her to her feet, studying her face for any signs he'd pushed her too far, too quickly. But one look into her eyes told him he'd been right in his original assessment. She was really into pain. He'd have to be very careful with his next choice. He was sure she wanted the St. Andrews Cross, but he wanted to save that for another time.

Another time? There it was again, the intense urge to see her again even before this night was over.

They'd never get through all those cards tonight. He'd be lucky if he lasted one more game. With that in mind, he looked at the cards on the table, studying them carefully before selecting the one depicting the spanking bench. As he expected, she looked over at the Cross then back at him.

"We'll save that, shall we?"

In a shaky voice, she said, "Yes, Sir."

He led her to the well-padded spanking bench against one wall and helped her onto it. Carefully constructed just for this purpose, it was covered in butter-soft leather with places for her head to rest and her breasts to hang free. He took his time easing those mounds into the openings made for them, kneading and caressing them as he did so. Unable to resist, he pinched each nipple, hard, as he'd done before. "Does that feel good, sub?"

"Yes, Sir." She ran her tongue over her lower lip, a little habit he'd noticed that teased his already painfully hard cock.

In response, he pinched them again, holding on a little longer this time. He had something specific in mind that would ramp things up a little. But first, he had to finish arranging her to his liking. Satisfied that her breasts were in place, he made sure her head rested comfortably on the pillow beneath it. Extending the armrests to either side, he fastened the lined leather cuffs around her wrists.

"I know you wanted the St. Andrews Cross," he told her again, "but I see how easily you take yourself into subspace. I'm not ready for you to go that deep tonight. I don't know how we'll manage, but I hope we'll have time together again. We'll save it for then. But I hope to make it up to you with this." He slapped each cheek of her ass again. "I promise you'll enjoy it."

When he tested her pussy, this time, she shivered at his touch and tightened her thighs against his hand, attempting to trap it there. He spanked her buttocks with his free hand, chuckling over her eagerness.

"I can tell you want to come, but you know we're not even close to my giving you permission yet. Nod your head if you understand me."

When she bobbed her head, he swallowed a smile.

Damn, she was hot. And he was more aroused than he'd been in a long time. Usually, it took him the entire time of the play session to get to the point he was at now. He wasn't sure how long *he* would be able to hold off here.

Opening the cupboard again, he removed a short paddle, a small bottle of oil, and two nipple clamps with weights attached. Kneeling to give himself access, he placed one clamp on each pebbled bud, tightening it until the flesh swelled and turned dark. The weights dragged each one down, increasing her discomfort. When he looked at her face again, he could tell she was well into subspace.

Good. Excellent. He wanted her to be there, the place where she gave him complete trust, where whatever happened to her was completely in his hands, and she had handed that privilege to him. It was a key element in a good D/s relationship, even a transient one. He hoped this one would carry over into more than just tonight.

One step at a time.

He was ready to move forward with this card trick.

Pouring some of the oil into his palm, he warmed it with his hands before applying it to her skin.

"I like the feel of your body beneath my touch." He bent his head so his mouth was close to her ear. "I'd like to stripe you all over with that flogger then rub spicy lotion into every place it struck. Have you done that before? Felt the extra sting from the lotion? Felt it all the way through your body?"

"Yessss." She hissed the word, her legs moving restlessly on the bench.

"What about the single tail whip? Have you had a Master pleasure you with that before?"

"Y-Yes, Sir. I have."

"Did you enjoy it?" He poured more oil into his palm and extended the area where he applied it.

His Queen nodded her head. "I did," she told him in a soft voice.

She was trembling now as he built the anticipation in her body. He covered every inch of her from her neck to her ankles, massaging in the oil and talking to her in a low voice. "Your pleasure is mine. You know that. Nod if you understand."

She gave one sharp movement of her head.

"Do you know why I'm applying this oil? I'm sure you do. Because when I'm finished, I'm going to paddle that beautiful ass of yours, and this oil will intensify every strike to your body."

He took his time, making sure he covered every inch of skin, not just the areas where the paddle would be applied. He oiled the crevice between the cheeks of her ass, probing gently at the puckered opening of her anus and smiling in satisfaction when the ingredients in the oil bit into her tender flesh. He smoothed it along the lower curve of her buttocks, the inside of her thighs, and then her vulva. She flinched slightly when the oil bit into her tender skin and her body clenched, then she seemed to just let herself fall into it.

Satisfied at last that she was ready, he picked up the short wide paddle and, without a word, applied it with force to her well-oiled ass. The sound of the contact was loud in the room.

"Ow!" The cry erupted from her lips, but she didn't try to pull away from it.

"Yes, that's it." God, her little cry excited the hell out of him. "Let me hear you."

He set up a rhythm, smacking first one cheek, then the other, watching the red spread over the surface of her skin and grow brighter with each application of the instrument.

"Ow!" she repeated. "Oww, oww, oww."

Her cries were just as arousing to him as the sight of her flaming skin and the glazed look in her eyes. With each blow, the heat in her eyes burned brighter and her breathing became more ragged. Tears ran down her cheeks, tracking through her mascara and leaving smudged streaks. He was mesmerized by the sight of her and the sounds she made and so filled with a need to fuck her, it took all his self-discipline not to throw the paddle down and take her.

At the count of twenty-five on each globe, he forced himself to stop, knowing to go further could take her past safe limits. She was truly in subspace, deep in her head, tears still flooding her eyes, her nose running as her body succumbed to the pleasure of it all. He knew the pain had released masses of endorphins in her system as well as a huge dose of adrenaline, ramping up the intensity of her reaction.

He couldn't wait a moment longer. He had to have her. Now. Had to feel that wet pussy clamped around his cock. Stripping off his clothes, he rolled on a condom, climbed onto the bench behind her and arranged her as much as the restraints would allow so he had full access. Gripping her hips, he positioned the head of his shaft at her opening and drove into her in one hard thrust.

"Ohhhhh."

The sound she made drove his lust even higher. There on that padded table, with her skin a bright red from waist to thighs, her oiled body glowing in the lamplight, he pounded into her again and again.

"Hold off until I give you permission," he said between gritted teeth.

He could feel the effort she made in the way she tensed her body, and finally he couldn't hold off any longer. As his orgasm gathered at the base of his spine and shot into his balls and then his dick, he shouted, "Come now, Queen. Now."

They exploded together, bodies shuddering so hard it was a wonder they didn't tip the table over. His cock pulsed inside her again and again until he didn't think he had a drop left. Even then, he held himself in place while she milked him and gripped him like a wet fist.

Spent at last, he leaned over her, resting his head on her back for a moment before easing himself from her body. He was surprised he could even move. It took every bit of strength he could muster to back off the table, but he knew he still had work to do. He was a good Dom, and it was time to care for his sub.

****

For a long moment, Nia wasn't sure where she was. She was conscious only of the intense burning of her ass, the little tremors still spasming in her pussy, and the pain generated by the nipple clamps that kept her on the edge of arousal.

She sensed Blackjack ease from her body and slip from the bench. She wondered if she could just stay

51

there forever, embracing the pain that consumed her, that gave her such pleasure, and carried her into a state that wrapped around her like a cocoon.

She didn't remember consciously giving over complete trust to Blackjack, but at some point, that was exactly what had happened. It wasn't just the adept way in which he administered pain or the way he coaxed such a response from her body. It wasn't even the craving for more and more of what he gave her, a craving that he wisely took control of and managed properly.

No, it was more than that. The instant they'd connected in the lounge, she'd felt an invisible thread linking them. From his first touch, something inside her that had been dormant for such a long time snapped to attention and whispered, *"This is the one."*

He was utterly attentive and caring as he eased her back from subspace, wiping her face, cleaning her eyes, her nose, and the smeared vestiges of her makeup. Cleansing her body with soft, warm, damp cloths. Massaging her muscles with healing lotion. Applying special cream to her abused nipples. Whispering soothing words to her as he brought her back to herself little by little.

As he cradled her in his lap, a warm quilt wrapped around her, feeding her sips of water, she thought she'd never felt so coddled in her life. She had allowed herself to fall willingly into subspace because she trusted him to catch her from the second she fell back down. She almost didn't want to return to reality, to herself, afraid it would break the spell.

Still trembling slightly, she leaned her head against his shoulder, suddenly realizing he was still naked.

"Where are your clothes?" she whispered.

He gave a soft laugh. "I'll put them on when I need them. Why? Are you tired of my naked body?"

She shook her head. "Not at all."

She reached a hand out from the quilt and smoothed it over the hard wall of his chest, loving the sensation of the soft curling hair sprinkled over it. She touched the curve of his jaw and the masculine column of his neck. He was all man, in every way. Yet not so macho that he didn't have the capacity for tenderness.

Good lord, Nia. You sound like a romance novel.

"Take a few more sips of water," he urged, holding the glass to her lips. "You're still shivering, still coming down from the high. You were pretty far out there."

She managed a tiny smile. "Yes, I was." She wet her bottom lip. "Thank you, Sir."

He nibbled the lobe of her ear. "My pleasure."

Knowing he was right, she continued to take minute swallows of the icy liquid, feeling it settle her system. He continued to cuddle her on his lap, his hands working her muscles and smoothing over the curves of her body. All the while, he whispered in her ear, soothing words, soft sounds, words to make her feel safe and cared for.

"I got carried away tonight," he told her, licking the shell of her ear.

"You did?" She turned her head so she could look at him. "I don't—"

"I don't mean with the flogger or the paddle. I pride myself on never going beyond what a sub can handle. But I had so many other things in mind. So many other cards to play." He nipped her earlobe again. "I wanted to fasten you to the St. Andrews cross, run the electric wand over your nipples and clit, and eat your cunt until you begged me to let you come."

A tiny jolt of arousal wriggled through her as the vision flooded her brain.

"I had an image of that single tail whip striping your fine ass," he growled. "Then I'd fuck you with the handle, maybe in your ass."

"Blackjack." She whispered the word.

"The card that showed the woman with vibrators in both her cunt and her ass? That's what I want to do to you." He brushed a soft kiss on her cheek. "That and so much more."

"I'd like that, too," she told him in a low voice.

"So…" He licked the edge of her ear. "Are you up for another card game tomorrow night?"

"Here? I'll have to ask Kelly to put my name on the guest list again."

"I can take care of that." He massaged gentle circles on her back, a motion that soothed her and made her burrow against him. "What about when we leave San Antonio? How long before you go back to wherever your home base is?"

"Sunday. I have to be back at work on Monday. What about you?"

"The same." He shifted her on his lap, easing her ass away from his thick, hard cock that again poked at her ass. "See what you do to me? I have to keep seeing you."

She bit her lower lip. "To keep playing the game?"

He brushed her hair off her forehead. "I don't want to get ahead of myself here, but I don't remember the last time I felt such a strong, instant connection with a sub. I know you had to sense it, too."

She nodded.

"We have a lot of cards to get through, Queen of Hearts. I want to take you to my club in Dallas. Maybe have you bring me to yours." He put his mouth close to her ear again. "I want to take you to dinner, get to know you, spend weekends with you."

Her heart stuttered. She wanted that, too, but hadn't dared hope. For the first time in forever, she wanted to spend time with a Dom outside a club, and it thrilled her that he wanted the same thing.

"I'd like that," she murmured.

"We have a lot of cards to get through," he reminded her. "Maybe they can even predict our future. One that keeps us together."

She gave him a saucy look. "I should tell you that, when I went to Las Vegas, I was a winner at Blackjack."

He laughed, the sound rumbling against her body. "You've won this Blackjack, my Queen. And I want to make sure you keep him."

"I'll give it my best shot." She smiled back at him.

"Starting with tomorrow night?"

She nodded. "Tomorrow night."

"And maybe every night thereafter." He cupped her head and turned it so he could take her mouth in a kiss both sweet and hungry. When he lifted his mouth from hers, she was breathless with the intensity of the kiss and warmed by the sweetness of it.

"Yes." She winked at him. "And maybe every night thereafter."

Texas Hold 'Em

Sage Drummond turned up the radio in her car and rolled down the window a little, just enough to let in some of the night air. She was far enough from Dallas that the atmosphere wasn't permeated with fumes from the big city. As her car ate up the miles on the interstate into ranching country, she could smell cattle, hay, and horses.

She was more than glad to finally be out of the rundown motel where she'd been hiding for a week. But she'd had to pick someplace where Andrew wouldn't think to look for her. Someplace that had units in the back where she could park and not be visible from the road.

Things hadn't started out that way. In fact, it had begun so normally she had been completely fooled by Andrew Lockner's attitude. He was smart, sexy, rich, powerful, and a much sought-after Dom. It was only later—too much later—that it occurred to her she never heard any of his prior subs raving about him. In fact, most of them seemed to have disappeared from the scene.

His behavior had changed so slowly and subtly that she hadn't realized it until it was almost too late. The level of control increased so insidiously she had been trapped before she was even aware of it. First, the exciting scenes at the club, with Andrew the attentive, inventive Dom, then the scenes at home where they could play their games in private.

Oh, yes, he had taken full advantage of their privacy. Like the night he'd made her sleep with clothespins on her nipples. She'd had to put cool packs in her bra for three days.

Or the time he decided she wasn't subservient enough and made her spend an entire twenty-four hours of the weekend on her knees. Naked. She loved pain at different levels. It kicked loose all her pheromones and made her crazy with need. But this pain had been so excruciating that it breeched all her boundaries and she nearly passed out from it. And Andrew, the slime ball, had slipped on his other face, running a hot bath for her and massaging her tortured muscles. She learned, after a while, not to beg for relief, because that only excited him more.

And each time he told her, in a deceptively calm voice, everything she had done to deserve her punishment, he had chipped away her sense of self-worth a little at a time.

As time passed, his control had increased until, before she even realized it, she nearly forgot who she was. Even her work had begun to be affected, as her boss was quick but kind to point out to her.

The day she had looked in the mirror and hadn't recognized the person there, she knew it was time to leave. How had she ever imagined she was in love with him? How could it be that by day she could be a top-notch marketing expert with a well-known agency and the rest of the time a cowering mess?

Still, leaving had taken more courage than she believed she had. She'd planned well, however, packing what she could when Andrew wasn't home. Clearing out her checking account. Tossing her cell phone and buying two burner phones. *Thank God for police programs on television!*

She was sure Andrew wouldn't try to find her. That would take more effort on his part than he would want to exert. No, he'd be on to the next unsuspecting sub, twisting her up in his silken web until she was tied so tight she didn't know if she could get out.

She had no idea where she was going to end up, she just knew it wouldn't be in Dallas. And as she drove, she thought about her options. She really loved Texas. Like so many people born here, it was in her blood, just as being a submissive was. Maybe in San Antonio, with its rich historical culture and its atmosphere so different than Dallas, she'd find what she needed—peace of mind, a great new job, and a Dom who respected her.

Because one thing was for sure. At some point, she would need to dip her toe into those waters again. Only this time, she'd choose more wisely, guarding both her body and her heart.

****

I can do this. I can do this.

Sage repeated the sentence over and over to herself as she walked from her parked car to the door of Rawhide. Dipping her toe in the scene again after months of absence had been a little scary. No matter how badly she wanted it, she hadn't been sure she could handle it after Andrew. However, she'd given in to the craving and taken a chance.

Rawhide had been recommended by the owner of her club in Dallas. Knowing he was familiar with her background, she was also aware he would fill in Reulas, the Dungeon Master, as well as Clint Chavez, the managing partner, so she could be properly cared for.

Reulas had made her feel at home right from the beginning. Safe. And welcome. Very welcome. That was the atmosphere he created, and she had no reason in all this time to believe anything differently. And he always took very good care of her, letting her visit and observe, making sure no one approached her unless she wanted them to. And each time she visited, she felt a little bit better about being there.

Her new life had turned out better than expected. Good job. Nice apartment. Even a few casual friends, although she was very careful not to share anything of her true self with them. People not in the life had a hard time understanding. She had thought about staying away from it completely, but it was so ingrained in her that she felt as if she was only living half a life.

Visiting Rawhide had taken courage the first time. The fear and diminished self-worth Andrew had left her with still clung to her, but it grew less and less each day. For three months now, she had come here once a week, sitting in the lounge, sipping a cold drink or coffee, and chatting with the members and guests.

She hadn't played in a scene yet. Tonight, she had finally decided it was time to step out of her self-imposed exile where active play was concerned. She wanted to submit, as if she'd been created just for this lifestyle. The big question was, could she after the damage Andrew had done to her?

"I will take very good care of you," Reulas assured her several times. "You are as safe in my hands as you will be with the Dom I will choose for you. Whenever you are ready."

She certainly hoped so. She wasn't stupid enough to believe she would find instant love inside the walls of Rawhide. She had made that mistake with Andrew, equating total dominance with total dedication. Then it had all fallen apart and left her running from an intolerable situation. She would be on guard that it didn't happen again.

Taking a deep breath and letting it out slowly, she pushed open the door and walked into the sensuous environment of Rawhide. Clint Chavez, one of the owners, saw her enter and greeted her with a smile.

"Good evening, Sage. It's so nice to see you tonight."

"Thank you."

"Reulas is waiting for you in the lounge," Clint told her. "He has a special evening planned for you."

"I'm looking forward to it," Sage replied. "Reulas is an excellent dungeon master."

And she was, albeit with a huge case of nerves. She stepped into the dressing room area and found a locker where she stashed her coat and purse. One last look in the mirror, one last fluff of her hair, a check of her bustier and thong, and she headed toward the lounge.

Reulas was leaning against a wall but came forward as soon as he spotted her.

"I'm so glad you didn't change your mind," he said, taking both of her hands. "I promise you won't regret it."

"I'm trusting you. I hope you know that."

"I do." He squeezed her hands. "And I won't let you down. Come. I have someone for you to meet."

"Already? I thought—"

"Thought what?" Reulas cocked an eyebrow. "That I'd just point out my recommendations to you and let you watch them at play for a while?"

She gave an unsteady little laugh. "Well, yes. I guess."

"If you're ready to move forward, Sage, then you need to take that step. If not, just tell me, and we can spend a pleasant evening with you observing. There is a performance scheduled later that you might enjoy."

Sage nibbled her lip. If she changed her mind now, when would she get the courage to do it again? She'd let fear keep her from the role of submissive too long already. She wanted this. Needed it. So it was time to take that step forward, and she trusted Reulas to have her back.

"No. I'm ready." She smiled. "Really. I've missed this, Reulas, more than I can tell you. And I have the feeling that, if I back out now, it will be a long time before I have the courage to try again."

"Okay." He dropped her hands and wrapped his arm around her shoulders. "Then come with me. I have the ultimate Texas experience for you."

"Oh?"

"I don't know how close to real cowboys you get in Dallas, but around here, we grow them authentic. And you'll love this one."

Sage gave him a tiny smile. "You said you would, and you always keep your word." She blew out a breath, calming the quiver of excitement wriggling through her. "So tell me about him."

"I've known Garrett for a long time. He used to rodeo but retired while his body was still in one piece. Now, he raises stock for the shows."

"Has he—" She cleared her throat. "Has he been living with a submissive?"

Reulas shook his head. "No. He didn't think it was fair to tie someone to him while he traveled the country. But now that he's settled down, he's ready for a more permanent situation."

"And he didn't have someone in mind?" she asked.

"Do you think I'd have arranged tonight if he did?" He clapped a hand over his heart and grinned. "You wound me, Sage."

"Sorry, sorry, sorry. I'm just…" She sighed. "Nervous, I guess."

"No less than I expected," he assured her. "But trust me on this. He's free, looking for just the right sub, and a longtime friend. And way better than that asshole who nearly destroyed you."

"Did you tell him all about me? You know…" She flipped a hand in the air.

"I thought it only fair, both for your safety and his well-being. He's looking for just the right sub."

She frowned. "And you think I'll fit the bill?"

"I think tonight will be a good chance to test that." He gave her a little squeeze and whispered in her ear, "I handpicked him for you myself. He's more than just an excellent Dom. I think the two of you will have great chemistry together. I don't know what will happen after tonight any more than you do, but I think it will be an excellent experience for you both."

"Then let's do this."

He led her past small groups of people, exchanging a word or two with some of them, until they reached the bar against the back wall. Although Rawhide had a No Alcohol policy, they did serve a variety of nonalcoholic drinks. The bar had become a comfortable place for unattached players to hang out. He nudged her all the way to the end, to the last stool and the man who lounged there comfortably.

The moment she laid eyes on the man, Sage felt a shiver race through her. She was shocked that he could arouse her that easily. She wasn't used to it. She'd been wary of the situation, unsure if she'd be able to handle it. She had no idea exactly what she'd expected, but Reulas had been right about one thing. There was definitely chemistry. Only that was a pale word for her reaction to him.

Her pulse began to beat erratically. Heat exploded in the air between them and trapped her breath in her lungs. Deep inside her, something throbbed and expanded.

She took in every sensual, hot inch of him. A royal blue silk shirt and dark dress jeans fit nicely on the broad shoulders and lean hips that defined his body. In a very unsubmissive-like act, she lifted her gaze to look directly into his eyes. Even in the subdued lighting, she could see the vivid blue of them, a deep color that matched his shirt and highlighted his narrow cheekbones, thick brows, and the black hair that hung just past his collar.

Omigod!

She wanted to lick her lips.

The first thing she thought was, *I am in trouble.*

The second was, *but wild horses couldn't drag me away.*

For one very brief moment, she clawed for the edges of her sanity, remembering how long it had taken her to get back to where she was now. *Remember*

Andrew.

But even in their most intimate moments, Andrew had never impacted her like Garrett did. Not even close. And mixed with all that hot emotion and erotic sensuality was a strange feeling that she wanted to step outside her self-imposed emotional boundaries. But did she dare? Could she take this chance? A better question was, could she not?

Reulas looked from one to the other, trying his best to hide a tiny knowing smile.

You knew this, Sage wanted to tell him. *You know me so well by now. You knew I'd react to him this way. What are you doing to me, Reulas? You know my situation.*

And so he did. A man she had developed such a deep friendship with, one she trusted so completely, made her believe one thing. He would not let her come to any harm, either physically or emotionally.

The erotic dream in front of her nodded at the two of them. "Evening, Reulas."

"Evening, Garrett," the Dungeon Master said. "Meet Sage."

His gaze traveled slowly the length of her body. He took in the sight of her breasts swelling over the top of the bustier and her cinched in waist, pausing at the tiny triangle of red satin that just barely covered her mound. She forced herself not to tremble under his close scrutiny.

Her thong was soaked with the sudden rush of liquid, and when his nostrils flared, she knew he'd caught the scent of her musk. Did he find it pleasing? Did he find *her* pleasing enough to take her back to one of the private rooms?

Lord, she hadn't been this nervous since her very first scene as a neophyte sub. And her trepidation wasn't just about her physical assets.

When he nodded at Reulas's silent question, she relaxed but just fractionally.

"Hello, Sage." His voice was deep yet soft, with a rich timbre that vibrated through her body. Her name sounded like music on his lips.

"H-Hello." God, did her voice actually waver? What would he think? That she might be too timid for him?

She expected Reulas had given the man every detail about her, but why hadn't he done the same for her? She had no idea what he liked. What he wanted. What appealed to him. Damn! She should have asked a lot more questions.

"I like the name." One corner of his mouth hitched up in a tiny grin. "And the rest of you. Although I can't quite see everything."

"I'm sure Sage will be happy to remedy that for you," Reulas said with a smile. He handed Garrett a key card. "Your room is ready when you are."

"Thanks."

Reulas nodded and walked away.

"Well, Sage." That warm voice brushed over her. "I think I haven't seen quite enough of you yet. Come here." He motioned for her to stand between his legs.

As she moved, her eyes automatically dropped to the significant bulge between his legs barely concealed by the dark fabric of his jeans. When she looked up, Garrett was watching her.

"People tell me I have more than my share." He looked directly into her eyes. "But I promise you'll be able to take it. Obey me, Sage, and I will give you more pleasure than you've ever known."

A shiver skated over her skin. "It will be my pleasure to serve you, Master."

"I prefer Sir," he corrected. "On the chance that our connection extends beyond tonight, you should start addressing me properly."

"Yes, Sir. Of course." The slight command made her pussy throb in anticipation.

"Let me look at you." He tugged on the lacings of the bustier, loosening them and finally pulling them completely free. The garment fell to the floor. "Leave it for the moment."

"Yes, Sir."

She stood completely still while he cupped and shaped her breasts with his hands, tweaking her nipples with thumb and forefinger, pinching them until she sucked in her breath. Sharp little arrows of pain shot straight from those pebbled buds to the core of her pussy, sending another flood of cream to her thong.

He exuded such an air of authority, of command. Not the arrogant one that she had come to realize Andrew wore, but one that came from inner strength, from being a good and respected Dom and having that confidence in himself.

Her nerves jittered for a different reason now. She was sure this man was used to accomplished subs, not ones that came with a boatload of baggage. What if she didn't please him? What if she turned out to be a total failure? What if she didn't and he wanted more from her? All of her?

Holy hell, Sage. Get a grip. Until five minutes ago, you weren't even sure you could handle submission again.

Garrett drew in a deep breath as he continued to pinch her nipples hard, his nostrils flaring. His gaze never left her face as he watched her reaction to everything he did. Was she fooling herself that this was more than just the testing of a sub by a Dom? Had she learned nothing from Andrew? God, she couldn't do that again, but the electricity between her and Garrett was so strong it threatened to buckle her at the knees.

"You smell delicious," he told her. "I can't wait to run my tongue through your slit and taste all that cream for myself."

His words made her tremble with anticipation. She had to curl her hands into fists to keep herself steady. She didn't know if people were watching them or what they could see, edged into the corner the way they were, but it didn't bother her. Many Doms liked to show off the assets of their subs, a silent bragging that they'd snagged a treasure. She was used to this.

"You may pick up your clothing and follow me." He rose from the stool and headed through the lounge, knowing she would follow him.

She trailed behind him as befitted a sub, but at the same time, she was conscious of the muted whispers and the hum of conversation. She would bet her last dollar that Garrett was one of the most sought-after Doms at Rawhide. That subs lined up for scenes with him. That being chosen by him was an honor. Everyone who had watched her sitting quietly these past weeks and doing nothing more than observing was probably wondering why on Earth he had chosen her.

Knowing that he had accepted Reulas's invitation to play a scene with her gave her confidence a boost.

She kept her gaze lowered as she followed Garrett down the carpeted hall to one of the doors. He unlocked it with the key card, pushed the door open, and motioned her to follow him inside.

Sage drew in a deep breath and let it out slowly. *Here we go!*

****

Sage had been in all the rooms in her Dallas club but never in one of Rawhide's rooms.

She peeked out from beneath her lashes, taking in her surroundings. The carpeting on the floor was thick and soft, the walls covered in a dark paneling. Along one wall was a tall armoire with its doors open to display a variety of toys and implements. She was sure there were many more, as well as other things like lubes, oils, and condoms in the lower drawers.

A St. Andrew's Cross took up one corner, with a large easy chair and a small fridge in the other. She also spotted a spanking bench and a padded table before the snap of Garrett's fingers drew her attention.

"Some things to get out of the way first," he said in that deep, liquid voice. "You may look at me while we take care of the preliminaries."

She looked up. "Yes, Sir." Automatically, she spread her feet wide apart and clasped her hands behind her back.

Garrett studied her face for a long time. What was he seeing? What was he looking for?

"I want you to relax for a minute, sub. We're going to take care of all the things dancing around in your brain." She nodded, and he continued. "Reulas told me about your background. He said you gave him permission."

"I did," she agreed.

"That was very smart of you. You left a very bad situation, one that can scar you emotionally as well as physically. I need to be able to spot signs that I'm straying too far into territory that might give you flashbacks."

"Thank you." Relief flowed over her.

"This is something a responsible Dom would pay attention to. It's important that you believe I fall into that category."

"Because Reulas told you about me," she guessed.

"No. Because it's who I am. I am a demanding Dom but at all times concerned with the welfare and safety of my sub. If there are things that I want and need, things that you might not be comfortable with, we can negotiate. In the end, we may discover we don't actually suit each other."

His face was expressionless, but something hot lurked in his eyes, something that reached into the deepest part of her. Sage didn't know if he had cast a magic spell, or maybe Reulas had, or whatever. She only knew that she felt a connection with this man that she didn't want broken. And whatever went on between them, she would not walk away from it.

"Well?" he prompted.

"I trust Reulas," she said, "so I trust you." And that wasn't the only reason.

"Fine. Then let's begin."

A fresh deck of cards sat on a small table by the door. Garrett broke the seal and fanned out the pack then turned back to Sage.

"This is a first for me, choosing different scene activities by using a deck of cards." He riffled them again. "Think they've got any ideas from Texas Hold 'Em in here?" He gave her a smile that reached into every corner of her body.

She smiled back. "Knowing Reulas, I'm sure there are."

He examined the pack, shuffled the cards, and stacked them so the edges were even.

"Okay, my little sub. In Texas Hold 'Em, each player gets two hole cards. That means you and I will each pick two cards the other person doesn't see." He handed the deck to her. "Subs first."

She was pleased to see how steady her hands were when she took the cards from him. Turning her back to him, she fanned out the cards on the table, face up, and studied them. After a great deal of thought, she chose two—a picture of a flogger and one of the St. Andrew's Cross. Then she stood there, not quite knowing what to do with them.

"Just put them there face down," Garrett said. "We'll get to those last." He held his hand out for the deck and made his own choices. When the four cards were sitting side by side, Garrett cut the deck. "I'll go first this time."

"Yes, Sir."

She lowered her gaze and placed her hands behind her back again, nibbling her lower lip as she watched him go through the deck.

"I don't want you to be nervous, sub. I am demanding, but I respect my sub's boundaries."

She started to relax a little more until she saw the card he had pulled out. All it showed was a long length of rope, deep purple, probably silk from the image. She sucked in her breath at the sight of it and took an involuntary step back.

Garrett reached out to steady her, his hand closing warmly and firmly over her upper arm.

"I know your history," he reminded her. "But the rope is important in play for me, so I want to make sure you aren't afraid of it anymore. It will be up to me, as your Dom, to teach you that it can bring pleasure." He tucked a finger beneath her chin and tilted her head up. "It's important to me that you trust me, Sage."

Her eyes widened. He'd used her name, not the designation. "Why?" The word was out before she could stop herself.

"I'm sure this sounds strange. Ridiculous, even. At my age, I have only been looking for a sub whose tastes are compatible with mine. Someone with whom I could have a lasting exchange of pleasure. Someone who would live the life with me at home."

"But?" She couldn't wait any longer for him to continue.

He studied her face for a long intent moment, as if seeking the answer to some unspoken question.

"Reulas is very good at identifying chemistry between people," he said slowly. "I'm not necessarily one for instant attraction. Been there, done that, got too many T-shirts." His eyes bored into hers. "You weren't looking for more than your first scene in a long time, right?"

"Y-Yes." Where was he going with this?

"Something happened between us the minute we set eyes on each other." He gave her a slightly crooked smile. "Let's go with it, girl. Maybe Reulas knows more than we do."

Sage knew exactly how she felt, but to think that it

hit Garrett the same way, too…

"If we're going to get through this scene and maybe think beyond that, you have to believe I will never abuse the privilege you give me. I will only give you pleasure." He held up the card, with the length of rope on it. "Trust me, sub. I promise you won't regret it."

She blew out a long breath. He was not Andrew.

Go with it, Sage.

She nodded.

Garrett put the card face up on the table and held out the deck to her. "Now, you choose one."

"Just one?" she asked.

He nodded. "That's one for each of us. Tonight, it will be about quality rather than quantity."

"But what about the hole cards?" She gestured to the cards lying face down.

"Those will be for next time." His blue eyes blazed like cobalt fire. "And I promise you there will be a next time."

Oh, God, she hoped so.

Wetting her lips, she took the deck, shuffled through it, and again pulled out a card that showed a woman on the St. Andrew's Cross being flogged. Garrett studied it, then nodded again. "That has particular appeal for you."

She nodded again.

"Then we begin. First thing. Safeword. I never play without one, even in private."

"Spice."

Garrett nodded. "Because sage is a spice. Very good." He gave her another long look. "This is your first time in a scene after what happened. If at any moment it overwhelms you, just say your safeword and we stop."

"But—" She nibbled her lower lip. "But what if—"

"That won't be the end." His smile warmed her. "We can go as slow as you want, girl. I'm in no rush. If it takes several nights for you to immerse yourself completely again, that's how we'll do it." He cupped her chin. "I want to find out if the unexpected spark is real or a figment of an overheated imagination."

She could hardly believe he read her mind. But then, Reulas would only give her someone who understood and respected where she was coming from. Another knot of tension inside her eased.

"Does that work for you?" he prompted.

"Yes, Sir."

"Then let's begin. Shoes off." His voice had deepened and become more commanding.

Sage stepped out of her shoes and nudged them to the side.

"Now the thong. Hand it to me."

Her hands shook just slightly as she worked the scrap of fabric down her legs and held it out to him. When he lifted it to his face and deeply inhaled her fragrance, she became instantly wetter and needy. She could hardly wait to be bound and helpless for him, feeling the sharp bite of the flogger.

She waited expectantly for his next instruction.

Another shiver slipped over her as he walked slowly around her, studying every inch of her. He cupped each breast, lightly pinching her nipples before sliding his hand over the curve of her ass. He let his fingers trail in the hot crevice between her cheeks, the touch so electric more of her cream flooded her pussy.

"Go to the cupboard and fetch the purple rope hanging there," he ordered. "And bring me a small bottle of oil from the top drawer. Jasmine scented."

Her hands shook slightly as she lifted down the rope, the woven strands silken against her fingers as opposed to the rough hemp that Andrew favored.

For one brief second, a flashback slammed into her, but she deliberately forced it away. This was Garrett, not Andrew. Tonight would banish the past from her mind.

Grabbing a bottle of oil, Sage handed that and the rope to Garrett, then stood with hands clasped behind her back, waiting for his next command.

****

Garrett was having a hell of a time keeping himself under control. The very last thing he'd expected when Reulas told him about Sage was to be poleaxed by a storm of emotion the moment he saw her. He'd listened to the Dungeon Master describe this very special sub, a woman who had been badly treated by her longtime Dom and was just now testing the scene again. She needed special handling, firm but compassionate.

He had not expected to fall for this woman—or any woman—at first glance. When he retired from the rodeo, all he'd hoped for was a sub with whom he was compatible, someone he could share his life with.

But this? This was like finding the pot of gold at the end of the rainbow.

Lustrous, golden-blonde hair tumbled to her shoulders, brushing softly against creamy skin. Hazel eyes flecked with gold looked up at him through the thickest lashes he'd ever seen. Ripe full breasts, tipped with rosy nipples, made his mouth water while he hands itched to trace the curve of lush hips and a well-rounded ass. Her beautiful cunt was completely waxed so he could see every mouthwatering inch of it. When he'd slipped his fingers into the tunnel between those sweet cheeks, the heat of her nearly burned his skin and his cock painfully demanded release from its restraint.

Tonight, he certainly hadn't expected to find a woman he wanted to take home and keep forever. By the look in her eyes, the same thunderbolt had struck her. But first, they had to get past the baggage she still carried, which is why he had chosen the rope for his card. He would use it properly, as a means to gain her complete trust, to show her how different this could be.

He'd make this work. Erase all the bad memories that lurked in the back of her mind.

"I like to oil my subs," he said at last. "It not only enhances every contact with the skin but eases the bruising." He nodded at the padded table, covered with a thick towel. "Climb up on there and lay down on your back."

Her movements were so graceful, although a little self-conscious, not unexpected under the circumstances. When she was flat on her back, hands at her sides, he allowed himself a moment to look at her again. Then he toed off his boots and socks, stripped off his shirt, and set all the items next to the big armchair. He had to keep the pants on, or he was afraid he might embarrass himself. It had been a lot of years since a woman made him so hard and so hot and so ready this quickly.

Uncapping the bottle of oil, he drizzled a little into the valley between her breasts then poured some into one of his palms and rubbed them together. With slow, sure sweeps of his hand, he began to spread the lubricant over her skin.

"Next time," he told her in a steady voice, "and I tell you again, there will be a next time, I'm going to fit a nice pair of tiny clamps over these gorgeous nipples. Every few minutes, I'm going to tighten them a little more until these ripe buds are swollen and dark with the blood constrained in them. Then I'm going to lock your wrists and ankles to the table and spend as much time as I want just licking and biting them until I make you come with just that alone." He gave her a hungry smile. "But not until I give you permission."

He could see a tremor of anticipation skating over her. The muscles in her tummy flexed as he rubbed the oil into them. When he eased his fingers over the waxed surface into the slit between her labia, the pulse at the hollow of her throat accelerated. Eyes focused on her face, he massaged the tender flesh, her cream blending with the oil. Slowly, he spread the lips of her mound and sucked in a breath as his gaze landed on the swollen engorged bud of her clit.

As he'd done with her nipples earlier, he pinched it, lightly at first then harder and harder. Her hands clenched into fists to hold onto her control as he worked that little nub, stroking and massaging it, pinching it hard then stroking it again. Tormenting her clit gave him a good indication of what her tolerance was for pain long before he picked up the flogger, and that was important for him to know.

Every muscle in her body signaled her arousal, the stimulation that was driving it toward climax. She had a hungry pleading look in her eyes, but as a trained sub, she had to know she had a long way to go before he would permit her relief. Tonight, he would find out just how far he could push her.

His oiled fingers slid easily into her hot channel, itself so lubricated with her juices that he slid in and out without a problem. He increased to three fingers and then to four, the fit tight and creating delicious friction. Her walls fluttered around his intrusion and clamped down on him. Her breathing ramped up, her pulse beating faster, until he abruptly withdrew his hand and gave her clit one more hard pinch.

"Turn over," he commanded.

Moving with lithe grace, she rolled over until she was on her tummy. Spreading her legs as wide as possible even before he ordered her to. She was definitely a well-trained sub, and he was furious at the Dom who had abused what she had to offer.

But lucky for me.

"Tell me what you like about the flogger," he said as he applied the oil to her back.

"I-I like its bite against my skin," she said in a shaky voice.

"Pain makes you horny?" he asked.

"Yes. Sir." She added the honorific as if for a moment she'd forgotten to use it.

"And do you enjoy it just on your sweet ass and thighs, or on other parts of your body?"

Her breath hitched slightly, probably as much from the way he was stroking her as from the question. "I like it…other places."

"What other places?' he pushed. "Your inner thighs?" He paused with his hand on the curve of one buttock. "Your breasts?"

"Yessss." She hissed the word.

He leaned down to put his mouth to her ear. "And

do you like to feel the handle of that flogger in your pussy, where it will get all wet with your juices? I'm going to do that, then lick every bit from the leather."

Again she quivered, an indication to him that she found both the description and the imagery erotic and arousing.

Garrett slowly oiled her legs, squeezing her thighs and the cheeks of her ass as he did so. When his fingers trailed into the crevice between her cheeks, she tightened her muscles. Then he watched her again force herself to relax, taking deep slow breaths.

"Is this something you don't like?" he asked. "It's important for me to know. Is this a place where you call 'spice'?"

She shook her head, but her fingers were still curled into her palms.

"Don't lie to me, sub." He smacked each cheek with the flat of his hand, hard. The flesh reddened to a nice rosy shade. He could hardly wait to see the marks of the lash on her body. "Yes or no? Spice or no spice?"

She drew in a breath and let it out slowly. "No spice."

"You know I'm going to fuck you in the ass," he told her. "Maybe not tonight, but eventually." And God, the sooner the better if his body's reaction was any indication.

"Yes, Sir."

He reached for the rope. "We're going to start with this so you will learn not to fear it." He glanced over at the flogger. "Good choices for a cowboy, you know. A rope and a flogger."

God, was that a little smile on her face? So she could be a tease, too.

"You know, Shibari—rope bondage—is really an erotic form of play." He lifted her so she was on her knees. "Some people have perverted it to create extreme punishment, and that's what your last Dom did. I'm going to wipe that out of your mind and teach you that this is an instrument of extreme pleasure."

Almost lazily, he drew the rope across her tummy and her breasts and wound it lightly around her neck before slipping it away completely. He walked around behind her, slid the rope over her shoulders and down her back before drawing her hands back and winding the cord around them.

"Stay still," he ordered.

Measuring the right length on the rope, he tied a knot, tested its strength, and slid the braided silk into the cleft of her ass, pulling the rope taut so the knot lodged itself right on her anus. He heard the hiss of her indrawn breath and waited a beat to see if she would protest or signal him to stop.

When she didn't, he threaded the length between her thighs, placing another knot directly on her clit before drawing everything tight again. The oil on the surface of her skin made the passage of the rope over it slick and easy.

Easing his fingers between the lips of her pussy, he smiled at how much wetter she'd become. Oh, yeah, she liked this when it was done properly. His goal was to make her crave it.

"Do you want me to stop?" He wanted to be sure he wasn't reading something into this or imagining it.

"No." She shook her head. "No, Sir."

Again, he cupped her chin with his large hand and tilted her face up so he could read her expression and look into her eyes. The eyes never lied. In them, he saw heat and hunger and need and yes, the connection he'd felt from the beginning. She wanted him as much as he wanted her. He was stunned it had all happened so fast, but he wasn't about to make a mistake and lose it.

He wound the rope intricately around each breast, tying off a knot in the valley between them before looping the end of it over her shoulder and locking it into the pattern binding her wrists. She was now completely immobilized and apparently very aroused by it if the rich scent of her musk invading his senses was any indication.

Sage held herself completely still, although he could see a plea in her eyes.

"Do you want to come, sub? Tied up like this?"

She nodded.

"Say it," he ordered.

She licked her lips. "I want to come. Please."

Garrett couldn't believe the overwhelming sensation of possession that gripped him. All his other relationships had been both temporary and transitory. And while he'd enjoyed them all, he'd never had the desire to take them to the next level. With Sage, he wanted to put his stamp on her, his brand, and never let her go. It wasn't just the sex, either. God, they'd hardly begun to scratch the surface here. No, it was that deeper connection that crashed into him the minute he laid eyes on her. He was going to make this work, no matter what he had to do.

He walked slowly around the table, studying her from all angles, his mouth watering at the sight of her. His cock strained against his pants at the image in front of him, begging for relief. Her small tongue came out to swipe lazily over her plump lower lip. *That's it.*

The table had a handle at one end that he turned to lower it so her face was even with his groin. Never taking his eyes from her, he shucked his jeans and boxer briefs, tossing them to where his other things were. Then he stepped forward, his hands cradling her face as he tugged it toward his engorged cock.

"I want to feel your sweet lips around my shaft, girl. Your tongue lapping the head. Your mouth surrounding it." He squeezed gently. "If you do a good job, I will reward you with an application of the flogger that will make you come harder than you ever thought possible."

She opened her mouth wide and slid his cock over her tongue, sucking in a breath when she closed her lips around it and gently scraped with her teeth. Then she did it again, and again, finally setting up a rhythm that drove him nuts. He knew he was big, a lot for her to take, but she managed better than he expected. She worked him with everything she had—lips, tongue, teeth, sucking so hard her cheeks hollowed out.

He closed his eyes, rocking back and forth, reveling in the heat of her mouth. He could have gone on this way for a long time, aroused even more by the fact that she was completely bound and helpless yet managed to serve him. The muscles in his lower back tightened, and the pressure in his balls intensified.

"I'm coming, girl." He got the words out through gritted teeth. "Now!"

His entire body clenched as he pulsed in her mouth, spurting cum into the back of her throat. To his amazement she swallowed it all, not spilling a drop. Licking him clean when he was finished.

Damn! He had a real treasure here.

Slowly, he eased himself free, his cock relaxing, gleaming with the moisture from her mouth. Just that sight made him want to do it again. *Next time. And many times after that.*

****

Discomfort radiated through in Sage's limbs, but it was nothing like the excruciating pain Andrew had delighted in causing her. She licked her lips, enjoying the aftertaste of Garrett's salty cum as well as the pleasure in his eyes when he saw her do that. In her sub training, she had learned how important it was to please her Master. It was the key that unlocked her sensuality.

With everyone but Andrew.

Andrew had nearly destroyed the pleasure submission gave her until she'd wondered if she'd ever want to be with anyone again. When Garrett insisted on using the rope, she'd had huge misgivings, but for the first time, she really understood why people said it brought so much pleasure. Even in the awkward position she was in, the placement of the knots continued to stimulate her. Every time she shifted, just the least little bit, they rubbed her erogenous zones and ramped up her body's need for release.

But nothing superseded the pleasure she got from making Garrett climax in her mouth. She was proud that she'd swallowed every drop. The look of pure male satisfaction in his eyes was her reward, even trussed up as she was.

She wondered if he'd slip his jeans back on afterward, but no, he stayed gloriously naked. It gave her the chance to admire his fine, muscular ass, his long legs with their ropes of muscles, his broad back, and his toned arms. A thin scar ran down the bicep of one arm, and another swirled on his right shoulder. His chest was covered with a mat of fine, dark hair, but even through the tiny curls she could see another long scar.

Rodeoing. How many times had he been thrown? Had he broken bones? She was thankful he hadn't damaged himself any more than that.

She couldn't help staring at his cock, enormous even at half-mast, as he stood before her to undo the rope. He unwound it slowly, taking his time, making adjustments as he went. She had thought he was going to remove it completely, but no, he had other plans.

By the time he was finished, it circled her body from beneath her arms to her hips, the knots on her clit and her anus still in place. When she moved, they rubbed against the sensitive areas, stimulating her even more. She was so close to sensory overload.

"I always take care of my subs," Garrett told her, lifting her from the table and carrying her in his arms to the cross in the corner. "Your pleasure is as rewarding to me as my own." He locked his gaze with hers. "Believe that, sub."

And she did, in her heart as well as her brain.

Very carefully, he arranged her face down on the cross, fastening the manacles around her wrists and her ankles, and smoothing his hand down the length of her body. She was riding the edge of release so tightly she had to grit her teeth to keep from coming. *Not until he gives you permission*, she kept reciting in her head.

But God, it was just so hard. The silken knots abrading her clit and her ass plucked at every overstimulated nerve ending. When he eased his hand beneath her head, she frowned, wondering what he was doing. Then she felt a long band of silk slip into place over her eyes. Blindfold! Oh, God! Without her sight, every other sense ramped up, eroding her control even more.

Next, she felt the smooth glide of the flogger down the length of her legs, tracing the outside then drawing a line up the inside of one thigh and down another. He prodded gently at her pussy, rubbing the knot of overheated flesh, pressing into it, then doing the same thing in her ass. When a moan escaped her lips, he did it again and again.

And without warning, the strips of the flogger bit into her ass. She jerked at the sudden sharp contact, causing even further friction with the knots.

"Ten strokes, girl." Garrett's voice was husky and taut with need despite his release. "Count them. Out loud."

"Ten," she said after the first full one fell. "Nine. Eight. Seven."

With each blow, the leather thongs kissed with the sharpness of a knife, again and again. Pain radiated from her buttocks and her thighs until, from her waist to her knees, she was one large area of heat and pain. And each stroke made her pussy clench, the orgasm deep inside her trying to claw its way out. She couldn't even squeeze her thighs together to control it.

By the time she got to one, she was afraid she would come without his permission, disappointing both of them. A good sub practiced discipline, and she wanted to be a good sub for him. Maybe more than she'd ever wanted to be for anyone else.

She heard the thud of the flogger as it fell to the floor. She waited, breathless for the words she so desperately needed to hear. The words of permission.

Instead, Garrett unfastened her ankles and wrists and turned her onto her back, mindful of the blazing soreness of her skin. Then he slid the blindfold off, and she blinked at the sudden light, even though it was subdued.

"Sir?" She would not embarrass herself by begging, but oh God, she wanted to.

"I wanted this since the minute I laid eyes on you," Garrett ground out.

In the next moment, he rolled on a condom, lifted her legs to wrap them around his waist, and drove into her, fully seating himself.

"Ohhhhh," The word came out on a sigh of pleasure.

"I'm going to fuck you, Sage. Put my stamp on you. People will see you and know you are mine." He slid back slightly and thrust in again. "We'll negotiate until you're comfortable with everything, but know this. I am not sharing you with anyone else. Not now, not ever. Any problem with that?"

His eyes burned into hers, and what she saw in them gave her such a sense of belonging, of completeness, she had no desire to object.

She managed a smile. "Not a one."

"Fucking damn right."

One more retreat and thrust with his hips, and with her heels digging into the small of his back and his hands braced on the table, he drove her to an orgasm that shattered her with its intensity. She had no idea how long they rocked together, shuddering, shaking, locked together in the intensity of the act.

When the last aftershock had finally subsided,

when they were both breathing somewhat normally, when her heartbeat had settled to a steadier beat, Garrett touched his forehead to hers.

"Mine," he growled.

She nodded, unable to form a sensible word.

Then he did the unexpected. He touched his mouth to hers, eased his tongue between her lips and kissed her with such intensity her entire soul was affected. He licked the softness inside her mouth, her gums, even her teeth, coaxed her tongue to dance with his and sucked it into his own mouth. When he broke the kiss, he traced the outline of her lips with the tip of his tongue, then took her in a kiss even more ferocious and possessive.

"Mine," he repeated. "And make no mistake. You will be cared for better than you ever dreamed possible."

She smiled, her body still trembling. "I believe you."

He frowned. "You do like horses and cattle, right?"

She burst out laughing. She just couldn't help it. "I do, but if I didn't, I could learn very fast."

He lifted her from the table and carried her to the big easy chair in the corner. First, he carefully removed the complicated arrangement of the rope. Then he fetched her water from the little fridge and a thick comforter from the drawer in the armoire. Holding her on his lap with the quilt around her, he massaged her arms and legs. When he was apparently satisfied she was back to herself, that he had given her proper aftercare, he set her down while he quickly dressed.

"I'm taking you home with me," he told her. Told, not asked. "I'll send one of the hands to get your car tomorrow."

"If I say you're taking a lot for granted," she teased, "would you give me another punishment?"

He stopped in the process of buttoning his shirt and grinned at her.

"You might turn out to be more of a handful than I expected."

"Could be."

She started to push herself out of the chair, but he swooped in and gathered her up again.

"I'll have Reulas get your purse and whatever from the dressing room. He'll bring the stuff straight to the truck."

Which was exactly what happened. The Dungeon Master had her things to them in just a few minutes. When he handed them to Garrett, he had a big shit-eating grin on his face.

"Damn, it's hard being right all the time," he joked. "It's a terrible burden to bear."

"But you'll manage," Garrett told him. "Right?"

Reulas nodded.

Garrett opened the driver's door, then turned to look at the other man. "Thank you for this."

"My pleasure."

"No." Garrett gave him a slow smile and trained his gaze on Sage. "I actually think it was all mine."

Dealer's Choice

Fiona "Fee" Wilder leaned back in her desk chair and raked her fingers through her hair. Her stomach felt as if a chorus line of butterflies were doing a hot jive in there. She'd waited all day for just the right moment to bring this up, and she wanted his full attention.

"Clint."

Her boss was still engrossed in searching for something in one of the file cabinets.

"Please pay attention. I want to talk to you about something. And it's important. Can you please stop a minute and pay attention?"

He turned to her and grinned. "I pay attention to you all the time. How could I help it, the way you order me around?"

Fee snorted. "That'll be the day. I'd like to meet the person with enough guts to give you orders."

He extracted a folder, closed the cabinet drawer, and dropped into the chair in front of her desk. In jeans and a T-shirt, his thick, black hair pulled back with a rubber band, he looked as far from the owner of an exclusive BDSM club as was possible. Hardly anyone ever saw him that way, but Rawhide was closed during the day. Usually, it was just the two of them. The cleaning service and the helpers didn't arrive until late afternoon.

Clint Chavez ran a tight ship. People who came to

Rawhide to play respected the rules or they didn't get to play again. But in the six months she'd been working there, Fee had discovered that beneath the face he presented to the world was a warm, compassionate individual, a person he showed only to a few select people. She'd give anything to know what his backstory was.

"Okay, what's so very important?" He nodded at her computer and the stack of folders on her desk. "Too much to do? You seem to be managing everything nicely."

"Of course I am." She glared at him. "Despite my excellent recommendation, you would have fired my ass if I wasn't."

He nodded. "The paperwork and booking records have never been in better order. And Reulas tells me you're becoming an expert at doing the membership interviews."

"I appreciate that. But…" She wasn't sure how to really tell her boss what she wanted. Would he turn down her request? Tell her she didn't know what she was asking?

"But what? Spill it. You have my undivided attention."

"You'll admit I make good choices here, right? Good decisions? Good suggestions?" She leaned forward. "Wasn't I the one who persuaded you to let Tanner Sloat introduce his card game? And didn't it turn out to be the success I told you it would?"

Clint rested one booted foot on the edge of the desk and used it to tip himself back slightly in the chair. He studied Fee as if analyzing every inch of her. "I do. So tell me what it is you're having such a hard time spitting out? I hope you aren't going to piss me off. You've made yourself so invaluable around here that I can't just dump your ass out the door."

She laughed. "You always try to sound so tough."

"And it works, too. With everyone but you. Come on, Fee. You've got me in a receptive mood. What's your heart's desire?"

She picked up a pen from her desk, fiddling with it to steady her nerves, and gave Clint one of her best smiles.

"I want to play at Rawhide."

"No." The chair legs came down with a thud. "Absolutely not. No way in hell."

"But why?"

He studied her with a look that made every nerve in her body tingle and flame. "Fee, just because you've observed doesn't mean you're ready to jump into the waters. There's a lot more involved than just playing in a private room for an hour."

She frowned. "Of course. I know everything that goes on here. It's hard to miss it. You invited me to the last three performance nights. You've even had me monitor the rooms occasionally. Didn't you think I have a natural, healthy curiosity about it all? Didn't you think I'd ever want to experiment with it myself? Be tempted by it?"

Clint reached across the desk and took one of her hands. "Fee, Fee, Fee. It isn't just the activities themselves. It's the state of mind. Inside yourself you have to have the desire to dominate or submit. You have to wonder how much pain it would take to raise your level of gratification. And the act of dominance or submission has to be what gives you the ultimate pleasure. It's the whole package."

"I know that." She bit her lower lip in frustration. "I haven't brought this up to you before, because...because..."

"Because what?"

"Promise you won't tell me I'm crazy? Or that I'm imagining things?"

He grinned. "I'll do my best, although you know I like crazy." Then his face sobered. "Just let it out, Fee. What is it that's got you so twisted in knots here?"

She looked down at her lap. "I think... That is, I feel... Oh, hell. The more I watch the subs both in the private rooms and on performance nights, the more I have this feeling inside me that I might be one."

Clint gently squeezed the hand he was holding. "Fiona. Look at me."

She lifted her gaze to meet his. "What?"

"You worked at a similar club before you moved to San Antonio. Did you ever have that same feeling there? That same latent urge?"

"Yes." She had to be truthful with him. "But not as strong as since I've been here. Besides, I thought maybe it was just the excitement of it. Something different. But I watch the women here who are subs and talk to them. And I realized that deep inside me I think I have the same desire for that domination that they do. It's just taken me a while to understand that."

He was silent for so long her stomach clenched with tension. Finally, he released her hand and leaned back in his chair. "You *think*. Isn't that what you said? *You think*? A big part of this is the psychological state of mind. Do you think your head is into it?"

She opened her mouth to say something, but he

held up his hand. "Let me finish. Think about this carefully, because I don't want you to make a mistake." He looked at her with his famous Clint Chavez stare. "We have neophytes come here now and then. You've taken their information. Are you telling me you want to explore your inner sub? Or find out if you really have one? Is that what you're saying?"

Fee wet her lips and tried to gather her thoughts. This unfamiliar need inside her had been plaguing her for months. It disturbed her at night when images from the club invaded her dreams and she switched places with the women in the scenes. It wasn't just that it made her pussy wet and her nipples ache with need. It was more than that, a deep-seated hunger that she was finally willing to embrace.

Could she make Clint see that? Would he honor her request?

"That's exactly what I'm telling you. I'm not taking this lightly. I want you to understand that. The more I see, the more I talk to people, the more something inside me is urging me to test this." She caught her bottom lip between her teeth as she weighed her words, then released it. "I've known for some time that something was missing in my sex life. I started to feel it at the club where I worked before. At Rawhide, the need became even stronger."

He watched her for a long moment. "So you've given this a lot of thought. Is that what you're saying?"

Fee nodded. "I am."

"Say I was to go along with this. Have you picked out a particular Dom? For a neophyte sub, that Dom needs to understand the basics of training and exactly how far to take the game."

Fee shook her head. "No. I thought I could discuss that with you. As a partner and the one who has hands-on management, I figured you'd be able to help me with that." Heat crept up her cheeks. "I, of course, want it to be someone I can, um, relate to."

He grinned. "Sexually."

"Yes." She buried her face in her hands.

She was stupid to even have brought this up. With a love life that became more boring every year, her inner self as well as her body had been sending her strong signals. She yearned to find the right Master and the right relationship. She wanted that power exchange, that complete trust she observed in the couples who came to Rawhide. Heat crept up her cheeks with the sudden embarrassment of the situation. Maybe this was a bad idea. Except…she really, really wanted it.

Clint pulled her hands away from her face. "Look at me. If you really want to explore these feelings, this is the best place to do it. In a private room with a Dom I've personally vetted. And with me monitoring the situation. That's the only way I'd feel even halfway comfortable with this."

She finally looked at him again. "Then you don't think I'm nuts?"

"Remember who you're talking to. No, I don't think you're nuts. And I'd much rather you explore these feelings in a safe environment than off with someone I know nothing about. I would never want you to do that. You know how dangerous that can be. So let's talk specifics."

Fee blew out a soft breath. "You'll really help me?"

"Of course. But be prepared that once you get into

it, you may decide it's not for you."

"That's why I need help finding the right Dom. Someone who can teach me and guide me so I can make that decision."

He nodded. "Someone who knows how to train and also when to call a halt."

Fee twisted her hands together. There was one other thing bothering her, one she'd tried to ignore while she was planning her conversation with her boss. "I guess I didn't really think about this until right now. If it's a club member, how do I act with him afterward?"

"You mean, because you work here? Because you wonder how he'll look at you?"

She nodded.

"These are all things to think about. If you'll be uncomfortable greeting him at the door or seeing him with another sub, maybe this isn't going to work. I didn't think you were looking for a relationship."

"Hell, Clint. I don't even *know* what I'm looking for." She sighed again. "I just know I have to try this, or I'll drive myself nuts."

"Good enough." He lifted one of her hands and kissed her knuckles. "Leave it to me. I'll find exactly the right person and set it up for you."

"Wow! An owner himself is doing this for me." She smiled, relieved, at least for the moment. "Thank you so much."

"No problem. I have to take care of you. How could I run this place otherwise?"

She actually laughed. "Probably very well, but I'd rather you didn't think so."

****

Cade Sullivan opened his front door and stared at the man standing there.

"It isn't that I'm not glad to see you, but hell, Clint, what brought your ass all the way out here to the country?"

Clint grinned. "Nice to see you, too. How come you're not out roping dogies or whatever you do out here?"

Cade burst out laughing. "For one thing, a dogie is a stray calf, and we try not to have too many of those. For another, with an operation this small, I have two men who can do the heavy lifting for me. And finally, there's only barn work to do today. I was just about to head out there when you drove up."

"Oh." Clint frowned. "If I'm keeping you from your work—"

"Always glad for an excuse to sit on my ass for a while. Besides, it isn't that often that I'm honored by a visit from an old friend and one of the Rawhide owners." He leaned back in his chair, his tone an indication he knew how out of the norm for Clint this was.

His friend gave him an easy smile. "I don't suppose you have a cup of coffee for a friend, do you?"

"I think I can scrounge one up." Cade led the way into the kitchen. "Still take it black?"

"I do. Some things never change."

"But I have," Cade told him. "So keep that in mind."

When they were seated at the kitchen table with mugs of a strong brew, he nailed Clint with a piercing look. "Not that I'm not grateful for the visit, but you never show up without calling first. I'm going to assume you didn't want me to ask questions first."

He sat quietly as Clint took a sip from his mug. The man was obviously organizing his thoughts. The two men had been friends since before Rawhide, and they'd seen each other through some tough times. He knew Clint had worried about him ever since the situation that made him stop coming to a dungeon and choose to live in isolation at his ranch. It seemed today his friend was determined to bring him back into the life.

Cade had been dedicated to teaching couples not just the mechanics of BDSM but also the emotional exchange, the power switch. Each session had been an emotional investment for himself as well. He always interviewed his students, meticulously assuring himself they were ready for the classes, that it was really what they wanted.

Clint was one of the few people Cade had shared details with when a private session blew up in his face. The Dom in training had shown his cruel streak, and the woman had totally freaked out because of it. Cade was shocked when the woman blamed him for the whole thing, told him he should have known her partner had a hidden streak of savagery.

Cade had pointed out she should have realized it herself since the man was her Dom, and she'd exploded in hysterics so intense they'd had to call for medical help. As if that weren't bad enough, the Dom had threatened to sue him.

After that, Cade had walked away from everything—the club, his classes, all of it. He questioned himself a lot, wondering if he'd missed signs he should have seen. It made him doubt his abilities to the point he turned his back on the whole BDSM scene. Clint had called him several times since then, but Cade wasn't ready to analyze the situation and get his D/s feet back on the ground.

But apparently, the man had decided enough was enough. "How are you doing these days? I don't get out here nearly as often as I'd like."

"I'm doing fine. Is this a welfare check?"

Clint chuckled. "No, although I ought to make one now and then."

Cade watched him over the rim of his mug. "If this is still about Lupe, I've put that all behind me. Done. Finished." Although the pain might never go away.

"Which is why you haven't shown up at Rawhide for months." Clint's words were edged with skepticism. "Yeah, that makes a lot of sense."

"Look." Cade set his mug down and leaned on his elbows. "The training academy was great for a long time. I enjoyed it, both the classes and the lectures. But it was time to make a change in my life."

"You were the best of the Masters. Since you closed your doors and stopped taking individual appointments, there's a big void in the D/s community."

Cade shrugged. "After Lupe, I lost my enthusiasm for it. And I wasn't sure how my students would react after a crazy woman burst into a session and threatened everyone with a gun."

Clint shook his head. "Not your fault. You had no idea how unstable she was."

"But shouldn't I, as her Dom at the time, have seen it? She was an extended project for me."

Clint lifted an eyebrow. "Maybe, if you had found a woman who was more than a project, things would be different."

"I doubt it. She blew up right in front of me, and I never saw it coming," Cade pointed out.

"I'm not sure anyone would have."

"That means I've lost my ability to judge properly," Cade argued. "How could I ever go into any kind of relationship again? I still keep thinking it was somehow my fault."

"Shit, Cade. No one else blamed you for it. You were the best. People keep asking if you're going to open the academy again. Life happens, and you have to start living it again."

Cade took a swallow of coffee. "Sorry, buddy. You know that's not in my game plan anymore."

"But you're not completely rejecting the D/s play or the lifestyle." The look on Clint's face was nothing short of sly. "Right?" When Cade didn't answer, he said, "It's in our blood, Cade. None of us can stay away from it for too long. So will you just listen for a minute? Okay?"

Cade nodded, prepared not to like what his friend had to say.

"On the drive out to the ranch," Clint told him, "I mentally ran through all the objections you might come up with and the possible answers to them. The problem is, I know your retreat from the scene was because of an emotional meltdown. I also know getting past that can be hard. But I truly believe I've got the medicine to fix it if I could just get you to agree."

"Is that so?"

"It is. Cade, it's time for you to join the living and get back into the lifestyle that's so ingrained in you. I have a woman I'm convinced is just the ticket for that."

Cade studied the now stale coffee in his cup. "What if it backfires, whatever this plan of yours is?"

"I'm trusting my gut on this," Clint insisted. "There's a young woman who works for me. She is sharp, sassy, and has been a real plus for Rawhide."

Cade looked at the other man, trying to read behind his expression. "I'm not sure I like where this is going."

"Just hear me out. She knows all about D/s. She's watched many performances on performance nights, and she also monitors for me frequently. I trust her completely."

Cade didn't say a word, just motioned with his hand for him to continue. He wasn't sure he wanted to hear what the other man was going to say, afraid it might break through his carefully crafted shell.

"We had a long discussion. She tells me she's recognizing submissive tendencies, that she's fascinated by the D/s play and wants to see if it works for her."

Cade waited a moment before speaking again. "You have other Doms at Rawhide who can train her. Pick one of them. You don't need a has-been like me."

"You're no has-been," Clint disagreed. "And you're the best trainer I've ever met. She's a very special person, Cade. I won't trust her to just anyone."

Cade was curious despite himself. "Oh? Special?"

"She's a very special friend who needs proper care and attention. I want this done right. You might as well say yes because I'm not leaving here until you do."

This had to be some damn woman for Clint to haul his ass all the way out here. She piqued his curiosity, but would she be able to break the hold the darkness had on him?

"I'm a little rusty, but I have to say, I'm curious

about a woman who would make you come all the way out here."

Clint grinned. "It's like riding a horse. Some things you never forget."

"I have some restrictions, though."

"So do I." Clint pulled out his cell phone. "Lay it on me."

****

"Can you tell me more about him?" Fee looked at Clint, trying to keep the edge of anxiety out of her voice. They were in the owner's private office where he had taken Fee as soon as she got there. "Why did you choose him?"

Now that the night was actually here, her excitement was blunted by a sudden attack of nerves. She wanted to know more about Cade Sullivan than the fact he used to conduct training classes and private lessons. Where had he been all this time? Why didn't he do it anymore? Why didn't he come into Rawhide?

"Fee." Clint took one of her hands in his. "Cade Sullivan is hands down the best trainer in the city. Maybe in the county or even the state. He let an unfortunate situation push him out of the scene, but that doesn't diminish how good he is. And I think you're just the person to tug him back in."

"Yeah? Why's that?"

"Because he does his best work with subs who are new to D/s and need proper training. He's solid, or I wouldn't trust him with you." He studied her face. "You know, if you want to change your mind, that's fine with me. This is your call."

She pulled in a deep breath to still the sudden attack of nerves and let it out slowly. She wanted this.

She really did. She'd thought about it for a long time, and she wasn't going to back out now.

Besides, she'd been so aroused by the expectation of what the night would bring she'd nearly made herself come showering to prepare for it. She *wanted* to be tied up. She *wanted* the pain of punishment. She wanted the satisfaction of extreme arousal she'd observed with members of Rawhide.

"I want this." She cleared her throat and repeated in a louder voice, "I want this."

"Fine. Then we'll do it. I reserved a room for the two of you. Took care of it myself. Reulas knows this is under my oversight. Cade's already there waiting." He gave her a reassuring smile. "And I had a special deck of cards made just as we discussed."

She gave him an impulsive hug. "Thank you, Clint Chavez. You're the best."

He chuckled." After tonight you may be saying that about Cade. Come on, let's go."

Fee smoothed her leather microskirt down with damp palms, adjusted the tiny halter top that did little except give the underswell of her breasts a place to rest, and moistened her lips.

I'm ready. She followed her boss down the short hallway and took in another steadying breath as he tapped on the door then opened it, and—

Promptly forgot how to breathe.

Holy Mother of God. Talk about sex on a stick. Every nerve in her body went on full alert. Her nipples hardened to painful points, and moisture flood her pussy. She'd heard about instant connections with people, had listened to women go on at length about how, the moment they laid eyes on their Master, something inside them just went *click!* They knew from that first moment that this was The One.

Fee had always brushed their comments aside. Who fell in love in seconds, anyway? She realized now, however, exactly what they had been talking about. With just that first brief glance, she felt a deep connection to Cade Sullivan. Whatever emotions had been dormant inside her for so long leaped to life and shrieked, *This is it!*

Cade Sullivan was on the far side of thirty-five, with enough lines in his deeply-tanned face to make it interesting. Thick, chocolate-brown hair was long enough to cover the nape of his neck. His square jaw and high cheekbones gave him a rugged look, but it was his eyes that trapped her, darker brown than his hair and framed by eyelashes any woman would weep for. All of it topped a body that was whipcord lean and muscular. He was naked from the waist up, the rest of him encased in pants of soft supple leather. And he was barefoot.

She had to stop herself from licking her lips. *This* was the man who was going to teach her about BDSM? Every erogenous zone in her body began to thump in response, and something buried deep inside her slithered up through her, waking long-dead emotions and desires. Would he take her beyond the simple exercises? Make her suck his cock? Or better yet, bring her to the edge of pain before thrusting inside her?

Stop it, you idiot. Put a lid on your daydreams. He's given you no indication he got that same instant Wow!

But holy hell, she could hope, couldn't she?

She had to remind herself he was just here to train

her. She was no more than a neophyte sub to him. Still, something instantly sizzled between them, and she wondered if he felt it, too, even just a little. He was certainly excellent at concealing his reactions.

She was afraid, the moment he ordered her to fall to her knees in front of him, she'd embarrass herself by climaxing.

Clint took her hand and drew her forward. "Fiona Wilder, meet Cade Sullivan."

Cade simply nodded at her, then looked at Clint. "Thank you for setting up the room as I asked."

His voice was deep and hoarse, like gravel rolling around in a steel drum. The timbre resonated in her body and set her pulse pounding.

"My thanks to you." Clint looked from one to the other. "I'll leave you both to it, then."

The door clicked shut softly behind him.

Fee didn't move, waiting for Cade to speak.

"Some things to get in front of us first," he told her.

She dipped her head. "Yes, Sir." She gave the honorific extra emphasis.

"I'm glad you're already aware of the proper form of address." One corner of his mouth twitched then firmed again. "Before we begin, I need to reassure myself that we should even be doing this. A lot of people are titillated by the thought of this, but the actuality is more than they bargained for. Clint tells me you know the basics, that you've observed and know exactly what it is you're stepping into."

"Yes. I do. I want this."

He studied her for a long moment, as if he could see inside her head. "Tell me exactly what it is you want from this. Or think you do."

She wet her lips and swallowed. She wanted him to really understand. "I want the power exchange I see between subs and Masters. The complete trust they give each other. I've never had that in a relationship. Ever."

He narrowed his eyes. "Is that all you're looking for?"

She shook her head. "I've watched couples—or groups—at Rawhide, been an observer and monitor at Clint's request. I see the pleasure those subs receive from the pain administered by their Masters." Heat crept up her cheeks. "Their sexual pleasure is obvious. I want that—the sexual gratification and satisfaction that is so obvious in their responses."

She lowered her gaze. "I want to feel for myself what head space is like. Vanilla sex has long ago lost its appeal for me. I don't just want this. I need it. Can you understand?"

She looked up again. Had she explained her reason for this in a way he could relate to?

His gaze focused on her, as if he were trying to see inside her head. "Perhaps it might be more than you bargained for. What then?"

She looked him straight in the eye. "Then I trust my Master to be aware of that and only push me as far as he thinks appropriate. I want to learn, Sir. From the best. And Clint tells me you're the best."

"He likes to brag about his friends." He dipped his head, as if reaching a decision. "One more thing. This is strictly a training session, a class where I introduce you to the basics of BDSM, and even more importantly, to the responsibility each person has to the other. We will explore your levels of tolerance for pain, what gives you the most pleasure, what turns you off, and most

importantly, the intrinsic key to a good D/s session—
the acceptance of the power exchange. No personal
sexual contact at all. I don't do that anymore."

She wanted to protest, to tell him he could do
anything personally with and to her that he wanted. But
they had just met, and she didn't want him to think she
was a simpering idiot. Maybe if this worked out and
they got together again… "I understand."

"All right. Before we begin. Safeword."

"Sureshot."

He lifted an eyebrow. "Strange word."

"It's from a favorite book of mine." She lowered
her gaze demurely. "It also describes the ability of the
man I'm looking for."

When she looked up again, Cade was doing his
best to swallow a laugh.

"Fine. Sureshot it is. I certainly admire your goals.
All right." He walked over to a small table, motioning
for her to follow him. "Clint had a special deck of cards
prepared for this session, but I'm sure he told you that,
right?"

"Yes, Sir."

"Fine. Next order of business. Submissives do only
what their Masters permit or order them to. Nothing
else. That's an important rule to keep in mind. Do you
understand?"

"I do."

"Good. Don't forget it. The deck Clint prepared
has the basics of training plus some introductory
activities. Come stand here while I open the deck and
we cut it."

She walked over to a place near the table and
waited while he unwrapped the deck, fanned it, and

shuffled. Then he put it down and waved a hand at it.

"Let's do this a little differently. We'll play Dealer's Choice. Cut the cards and deal a hand to each of us. You will choose first."

Hands trembling only slightly, she did as he ordered and dealt out five cards to each of them. Hoping she was making correct choices, she pulled out a card and placed it so he could see it.

Cade lifted an eyebrow. "Blindfold?"

"I've done a lot of reading. I understand that when you remove the sense of sight, all the others become stronger. More intense." She caught her bottom lip between her teeth. "I want to feel everything as intensely as I can."

He made no comment, simply took two cards from his hand and put them down next to hers.

"Two choices. You pick."

She looked at them and shivers raced through her body. The pulse in the walls of her pussy intensified, and her breasts felt heavy. She selected the one with a kneeling sub, naked and handcuffed, heavy clamps tugging on her nipples. She watched for Cade's reaction.

He said nothing, just pointed to her hand, indicating she should choose another.

This time, she extracted one that showed a sub on a spanking bench, legs wide apart while her Master administered the punishment. The artist had captured the look of intense pleasure on the sub's face.

By the time there were ten cards on the table, Fee was on the edge with anticipation. Cream from her cunt wetted the inside of her thighs. She wanted to tear off her clothes and rub them and herself all over the man sitting across from her.

This was going to work! What naughty things could she do that would make him order her to her knees, cuff her wrists, and paddle her ass until it stung and cream dripped from her pussy.

Cade shifted his gaze back to the cards, rearranging them before he turned that hot, powerful gaze on her. "Take off your clothes and place them on the chair by the wall. Then stand in the center of the room."

Showtime!

Fee was out of her clothes in seconds, pleased at the steadiness of her hands as she completed her task despite all the thoughts whirling in her imagination. She had worried she might feel uncomfortable with a strange man if she was completely naked, but instead, a shiver of excitement raced over her. Even before he said anything else, she was absorbed by what was about to happen.

From the corner of her eye, she saw Cade lift something from the cabinet built into the wall.

"You understand," he said with his back turned to her, "that you do nothing unless I order you to. And whatever I say, you do without question."

"Yes, Sir."

"I prefer Master," he told her.

For some reason that honorific sent a shiver of delicious anticipation skittering over her skin. Maybe it was the connotation of the word as opposed to Sir.

"Yes, Master."

"Good. Hands behind your back, feet apart, eyes closed."

She took another calming breath as she did what he ordered and waited for what came next. She knew when he was behind her, not just from the soft sound of his feet in the thick carpet but because whatever acutely male soap or aftershave he used suddenly invaded her senses and made her pussy clench in response. God, he smelled so good.

He's your trainer, not your Dom. Control yourself.

"Do not open your eyes, sub." He gave the order in a deep, controlled voice that set heat rushing through her.

In another moment, she felt the kiss of smooth silk against her eyelids as he positioned the blindfold in place and secured it at the back of her head. Then she heard the click of a lock and felt the touch of steel as Cade fastened manacles around her wrists.

"Spread your legs wider. It will help with your balance." He touched her shoulder. "From this point forward, remember, you do only what I tell you to and you do it all. If something is beyond your comfort zone, use your safeword. Otherwise, I control your every movement. Nod your head if you understand."

She dipped her head once then widened her stance, adjusting her balance.

"You were right about the escalation of the remaining senses when one is removed. You will feel this a lot more if you can't see what I'm doing."

In a sudden move, he grasped both nipples between his fingers and squeezed, gently at first then exerting more and more pressure. She sucked in a breath as the pain increased, but then the heat bloomed again and, with it, a powerful, sexual need.

"These are mine to do with as I wish." His tone was mild, as if they were having a conversation, but she heard the steel of command beneath it. "Right now, I want to pinch them until they turn deep red, like they just did."

Suddenly, his touch was gone, and she waited for what came next. Oh, yes, the clamps. She'd selected that card.

The press of metal against her nipples shocked her with cold, but as Cade tightened first one then the other and the heavy weight dragged her nipples down, the throbbing in her inner walls intensified.

"I can smell how aroused you are." He could make her come with his voice alone. "Remember the rules. You do only what I order you to or give you permission for. Do not come without my consent. Break a rule, this session is over."

No. She didn't want it to be over. She wanted to stay in this room with him forever.

Damn, Fee. What the hell is going on with you?

She bit the inside of her cheek in an attempt to control her unexpected rush of feelings.

"Empty your mind of all thought." His words were like a sharp knife to her brain, as if he knew what she was thinking. "Feel, sub. Do nothing but feel." He was so close behind her the crisp hair on his chest brushed her shoulder blades.

When he moved his lips close to her ear, she felt his warm breath as he whispered, "Ready for heat?"

She dipped her head once, readying herself.

He touched her shoulder first with his fingertips, then with—not heat but cold! Icy, icy cold! She'd read about this, where Doms teased their subs, alternating hot and cold but never letting them know for sure which they were getting next. She sucked in a breath.

"Again," he whispered.

This time it was heat, just the barest prick of it from a battery-operated wand. He alternated the sensations but not in any pattern that she could anticipate. She soon lost count of the number of contacts, her awareness softening as a cloud of sensation shrouded her brain. Subspace. Had she reached it already? How was that possible?

"Stand straight." Cade's words cracked like a whip, shocking her back to the present.

Fee hadn't even been aware she was slouching. She lifted her head, threw back her shoulders, and moved her feet a little farther apart for balance. The alternate sensations of hot and cold still tingled through her. If this was a Dom she'd played with before or if she were a regular at the club, her Master would begin testing her readiness now by running his fingers along the length of her dripping slit. Perhaps even sliding one or two fingers inside her hungry sheath.

But tonight, he was the teacher, so she didn't expect personal contact. But she wanted it, craved it.

Without warning, he touched one of the wands to a cheek of her buttocks, cold, twice, then heat. He did the same with the other cheek, although not with the same pattern. Then she sensed him move around in front of her, and in a second, ice cold touched the tip of one tormented nipple.

"Don't move," he warned her. "Stay absolutely still."

Did he know how hard it was? Of course, he did. But he was testing her ability to obey orders at all costs.

"Yes, Master."

She waited for another touch, another sensation, but nothing happened.

"Are you enjoying your fantasy, girl?"

She blinked behind the blindfold. What?

"Uh, yes, Master. But—" She bit her lip, a nervous habit she was desperately trying to break.

"But what? I give you permission to tell me."

"But I want it to be more than a fantasy."

His laugh had a rusty sound. "You've barely begun. Don't you think you should wait at least until the session is over before saying that?"

"If you say so." She paused. "Master."

"Feisty little thing, aren't you? I'm beginning to think taking you on as a fulltime project would be interesting."

Oh, yes, please.

"But I gave up on those." His voice had a closed-off, tight sound to it. "So let's proceed." He dragged the tip of the ice-cold metal across her shoulders.

Fee stood, legs braced, waiting. When he touched the cold to her chin, this time, she jerked her head. Cade gripped her jaw with his fingers.

"Perhaps you'd like to feel this other places, too, girl." She felt his arm against her body. "Like here." The icy cold touched her cunt. "Or here again." He touched a nipple. "You chose the card depicting Florentine flogging. Did that appeal to you?"

She nodded, his fingers still tight on her jaw, her skin jumping from the flurry of alternating sensations, her nipples aching painfully from the heavy clamps dragging them down.

"That's a good type of play to move on to."

"Y-Yes, Master." She could hardly get the words out.

With a slow move of his hand, he slid the cold

instrument between her legs, drew it through her slit, and then away.

"Damn, girl. You're very responsive. A good choice for this." His words wrapped around her like a warm blanket.

She wanted to tell him she was responding as much to him as to what he was doing, but she waited, her mind drifting, for the next assault on her senses. Was he getting the flogger? But she'd quickly lost the ability to think for herself or make decisions.

A good Dom will do that for you, lead you into subspace, and make safe decisions for you.

She tried to make her brain work, to visualize the flogger and the scenes where she'd seen it used. While she was struggling, her nerves still jumping from the hot and cold play, a bundle of leather straps struck her ass.

"Don't move, girl." His voice was firm, harsh even. "Remember. Not one movement at all."

Yes, she understood, but damn, it was hard. She had watched Florentine flogging before, two bundles of leather straps with bound handles, applied in a figure eight movement. She tried to concentrate, but the steady strikes of the leather soon had the last vestiges of conscious thought disappearing. Up, down, circular, one after the other so it soon became one continuous sensation. Heat blazed over every surface of her skin, and it became increasingly difficult to maintain her balance.

When Cade stopped suddenly, she wanted to cry out, but she knew it was not her place.

"Stand completely still," he ordered.

In a moment, a leather strap encircled her waist,

and a clamp bit into the fabric. He gave it a slight tug. She knew what this was. A metal twine hung from the ceiling, locking onto the belt, holding her more firmly in place as she lost the ability to control her balance.

The flogging began again, and this time, she just fell into it, her cunt pulsing, her breasts throbbing, her skin on fire. More than anything, she wanted the release of a climax, but he had not given her permission. Instead, she gave up fighting at all and just let sensation take her.

At some point, the pattern of flogging stopped, but it took her a moment to realize it. She was vaguely aware of the belt around her waist being released, the handcuffs unlocked. Next to go were the clips. Pain shot into her nipples as blood rushed into the abused tips. Then Cade was lifting her, carrying her. He wrapped something warm around her and sat her in the big armchair at one side of the room.

When he removed the blindfold, she blinked at the sight of him crouched in front of her. He was using the scarf to blot her cheeks. She was embarrassed, unaware she had even been crying.

He fetched a bottle of water from the tiny fridge and fed her small sips, urging her to drink slowly. She let him feed her the cold liquid, still struggling to cast off the cocoon of subspace. As she drank, he studied her face, a strange look in his eyes.

At last, he nodded, apparently satisfied that she was all right, albeit tired. And did he also know she was acutely sexually aroused? What was she supposed to do about that?

"Do you know that you are a born submissive?" he asked her. "Oh, maybe not outside the bedroom or possibly in the privacy of your own home. You're so responsive, so giving of your body, so—" He shook his head. "You should be careful who you play with, Fee. Let our friend Clint choose your Doms for you if you go further with this."

"We're done?" She frowned. "We didn't get through all the cards."

He just shook his head. "I'm going to rub a soothing balm into your skin as soon as I think you're recovered enough. And I'll give you some cream to treat those nipples with. They'll be sore for a few days. I'm actually not sure I should let you drive home."

"I'll be fine if you just give me a little more time," she protested.

His mouth crooked in a grin. "Arguing with your Master? You're not being a good little subbie."

"But—"

He touched the tip of one finger to her mouth. "Hush. Let's get you taken care of and dressed, and I'll discuss it with Reulas."

"I want to have another session with you." The words burst from her mouth before she could stop them.

That closed off look washed over his face again. He said nothing, just shook his head and went to fetch the cream for her body. He said nothing else while he tended to her, and she was wise enough to know she should just shut up. At least for right now. She'd talk to her boss tomorrow.

When he was finished and she was dressed, he left the room for a moment. While she waited for him to return, she tried to carve every moment of the evening into her brain. As abbreviated as it was, it far exceeded her expectations. She was sure a lot of that had to do with Cade himself. She had to find a way to get his story from Clint.

The door opened, and he was back in the room, her purse dangling from his fingers.

"I'm driving you home. Clint will follow and bring me back for my truck." When she started to protest again, he shook his head. "You're still unsteady. And still my responsibility. Take orders like the sub you want to be. Give me your keys."

Clint smiled and winked as they all proceeded out the back door, but he didn't say anything. Neither did Cade. In fact, he was completely silent on the drive, so she held her silence, too.

When they arrived at her house, he fiddled with the keys to find the one for her door and ushered her inside. When he handed the keys back to her, he stroked his fingers once down her cheek.

"Will we have another session?" she asked.

"I don't think so, Fee." He caressed her cheek again, his eyes filled with sadness. "I wish we had met a long time ago, little sub. Then maybe—" He shook his head. Then he put his mouth close to her ear. "You have my permission to bring yourself to climax."

Then Cade was gone, and Fee was left with a cauldron of emotions bubbling up inside her.

****

Cade had slept restlessly since the session with Fee, her image invading his dreams, her mouthwatering body, her embracing the role of a sub, her willingness to do anything he asked. One moment, he wanted her in his bed and in his life. The next, all the doubt of the situation with Fee rolled over him.

Okay, he wasn't a cruel Master, and he'd handled

Fee with the respect she deserved. But had she gotten the pleasure out of it that he wanted her to? Was the session all she'd hoped it would be or had he in some way disappointed her and turned her away from the life?

The damnedest part was, he wanted to see her again and maybe not just at Rawhide. What the fuck was up with that?

Now, he looked at the man sitting across the kitchen table from him. Maybe he should just toss his old friend Clint out and go back to his isolated existence.

Except once he'd tasted the sweetness that was Fee and allowed himself to think of the possibilities, could he even do that? He wanted this, and yet at the same time, it scared the shit out of him—the big bad Dom—that he might fuck it up. Better to play it safe and wallow in his miserable existence.

"I never should have let you talk me into that," he said, so many emotions still swirling in his system. "I knew it was a big mistake."

Clint smiled. "She got to you, right? I knew she would."

"So you set me up." He shook his head. "Why didn't I see it from the beginning? A fresh sub. New to the lifestyle but eager for it. Warm and giving."

"And certainly stable, or I wouldn't have her working for me," Clint pointed out.

Cade pushed away from the table and took both coffee mugs back to the pot for a refill. "A temptation, right? To seduce me back into the scene?"

Clint took the mug from him and shook his head. "More than that. She's exactly what you need to bring you back to life."

"There's nothing I need," Cade insisted. "I'm alive. I'm just fine. I'm happy with my cows. When they misbehave, I just take out the whip."

Clint grinned. "You could do the same with Fee."

Cade gave him a hard look. "I hope you reinforced what I told her—that I wasn't planning on another session with her. Fee is young and unspoiled and not one for a damaged old man like me to get near."

"First of all, she's older than she seems." Clint cocked an eyebrow. "How old do you think she is, anyway?"

Cade shrugged. "Twenty-four or twenty-five."

"She's thirty-two, asshole." Clint laughed, obviously amused at the stunned look on his face. "Secondly, she's exactly what you need. Forget about training again, unless you decide to reopen academy classes. Let this relationship develop.

"I know she connected with you on a really deep level. She didn't say so, but everything she's said and done since then has been like a neon sign pointing in that direction. She's certainly done her damndest to get your story out of me and persuade me to set up another session."

Cade shook his head. "You can just tell her no dice. We're once and done."

"Cade." Clint heaved a sigh. "She's exactly what you need. And unless I'm wrong, which I'm not very often, you have some feelings for her. I can tell by the look in your eyes, not to mention a muscle twitches in your cheek every time I say her name. I know you, old friend, all the signs, so don't think you can fool me."

Cade glared at Clint. This couldn't work. Not in a

million years. No matter how great that session had been, he still was, and always would be, damaged goods. "It won't work. Anyway, it's probably just some stupid crush."

"This is no crush, Cade." Clint leaned forward, forcing Cade to lift his gaze and look at him. "I could tell right away how you felt when you gave me a report on the session so don't try bullshitting me. Both of you are very important to me. I've been in this business long enough to see when people meet that one person who can complete them, and I see it here."

"Fuck, Chavez," Cade growled. "You sound like a goddamn romance novel."

Clint laughed. "Maybe. But I'm telling you the truth, even if you don't want to hear it. Do both of you a favor and see where this takes you. The journey can be as rewarding as the destination."

Cade hated to admit his friend was right on more than one count. Fee Wilder had definitely gotten to him in a very short time and in a way no other woman had. Ever.

His dreams every night has been filled with images of her luscious body, her unrestrained responses. Shockingly, his heart had responded to her as much as his body, although he'd sported a perpetual hard-on since that night.

He'd give anything to see where things went with the two of them. But history made him leery of stepping into another relationship of any kind. And to set up another training session for her… That would be just asking for trouble. When he walked away—and he knew he would because he was too damaged to do anything else—the pain would be too sharp for both of them.

"Forget it. I'm sorry you took the trip out here for nothing. It was a waste of your time."

Clint studied him for a long time. "Listen to me, Cade. You're my oldest friend. I know you probably even better than you know yourself. Let me tell her your history, so she won't be walking into something blindly. But give it a try. You'll regret it forever if you don't."

Cade stared into his coffee mug, trying to give his friend some reasonable objections. But all he could see was Fiona Wilder's face, eyes softened from subspace, body flushed with desire, cheeks damp from tears of pleasure. She'd been the only thing on his mind since he left her at her door. Had she pleasured herself the way he'd told her to? He wanted to call her and ask her to tell him about it in intimate detail.

Who was he kidding? He wanted her in his house, in his bed, in every room. Naked, on her knees, bent over his lap, a million different ways. Could he take the chance? Would it blow up in his face?

Finally, he drained the last of his coffee and pushed the mug aside. "Let me think about it, okay? I'm not saying no, just that I want some time."

"Fine. I'll give you until the end of the week. But if I don't hear from you by then, I'm bringing her to your front door and leaving her there. You won't turn her away. I know it."

Cade sighed. He knew his friend would do just that. Somehow, he'd have to figure a way out of this situation. "Okay. The end of the week."

Even as he said the words, a knot formed in his stomach. Was it possible this could work? That Fiona

Wilder could bring him back from emotional death? Was he even ready for it?

He'd spent so much time after the disaster questioning himself both as a teacher and a Dom. If he was making a mistake, it would end up badly for both of them. He guessed he'd have to trust his friend to know what was right.

****

Fee turned off the ignition and sat in her car, not yet making a move to get out. Since her long talk with Clint, she'd been by turns excited and nervous, sometimes even fearful. The brief session she'd spent with Cade only reinforced her belief this was real.

She'd thought long and hard about coming here today to Cade Sullivan's ranch. But the story Clint had told her, plus his long history with the man, had made her take the chance. It might not work out, but she'd never know if she didn't try. The truth was, she'd met a lot of men she wanted to have a deep connection with, but something had always been missing.

It wasn't just admitting she'd discovered her inner sub. Clint could have paired her with any Dom he trusted, and the night would have been great but would have lacked the incredible chemistry she felt with Cade. No, it was the man himself, combined with her new knowledge of herself.

Now, she was about to take another very huge step, and those familiar butterflies in her stomach began beating their wings double time. She drew in a long steadying breath, let it out slowly, and got out of the car. She had brought a small overnight case per Clint's "Just in case," but she set it down. She wasn't even sure she'd need it. First, she had to make sure the man would even let her in the door.

She checked herself over, brushing imaginary specks from the hip-hugger shorts and tank top she wore, smoothing her hand over her hair. Then, gathering her courage, she mounted the three steps to the front porch and rang the doorbell.

When Cade opened the door, she just stood there, staring. He was just as erotically handsome as she remembered. The T-shirt and jeans did little to disguise the exquisite masculine body she remembered, and his coffee-dark eyes were just as penetrating.

But more important, the electric sizzle between them still snapped in the air. And by his expression, he felt it, too.

He studied her for so long she wasn't sure he'd let her in. She could almost feel the tension vibrating from him. Then he stepped back and motioned her into his house.

"Clint assured me you'd be expecting me," she said nervously. Then she gave a tiny smile. "Master."

His lips twitched as he did his best to suppress a grin. "Ah, yes. Clint Chavez. My old friend. Should we call him the master, also? Master manipulator?"

Fee clutched the strap of her purse. "If this is a bad idea—"

He held up a hand to cut her off. "We won't know that until we give it a try, will we? Come in."

She followed him through the house, down a short hallway, and into what was obviously the master bedroom. The focal point of the room was an oversized bed, flanked by polished oak nightstands.

"You brought an overnight case with you?" he asked.

She nodded.

"We'll bring it in later."

"Just like that?" she asked. "I mean—"

God. Could she sound any more like an idiot?

He walked over to stand in front of her, hands on her shoulders. The touch of his fingers burned into her skin. "We spent one hour together, Fee. I shock myself by admitting you affected me as no other woman has for a very long time.

"I know Clint told you my story. Maybe he's right, that I'm finally ready to move on and that you're the one I'm meant to move on with. In that one short hour together, I felt more alive than I have for a long time. Our friend tells me you have similar feelings. He's persuaded me to see if this works." He smiled. "I want that if you do."

"Yes." Her heart was beating so hard she was sure he could hear it. "I want that, too."

"Then we shouldn't waste any time. Let's find out if Clint is right." He took a step back. "From now on, you are completely my sub. You will do whatever I tell you. If something makes you uncomfortable, tell me and we'll negotiate. Understood?"

"Yes, Master."

"I can't create the kind of situation I'd really like, because I have hands that work for me who come to the house off and on. That prohibits me from ordering you to leave off all your clothes except when we go out." He locked his gaze with hers. "That works well since I'm not as addicted to every aspect of D/s as some Masters are. I like a certain amount of independence and intelligence in my sub. But in this room, I am in charge. Understood?"

She nodded again.

"Excellent. You brought the cards?"

"Yes. I did." She set her purse on the dresser and removed the cards they hadn't used the last time, fanning them out on the hard surface.

"Dealer's Choice, just like the last time," he told her.

With a hand that shook only slightly, she pulled out two cards. One showed a woman on her knees, handcuffed, a man's cock in her mouth, a butt plug inserted in her ass. The other showed a woman on her hands and knees, blindfolded and gagged, a man behind her with his cock in her. Beside them, as if tossed after their use, lay a coiled long tail whip and a paddle.

Cade narrowed his eyes. "You're sure?"

She dipped her head once in acknowledgment.

"All right, but there's one thing I want to do first. I haven't wanted this for a long time. It's too personal. But I'm ready to chance it with you."

He cupped her cheeks in his work-roughened hands, tilted her face up to his, and took her mouth in a kiss so rough and hungry and demanding it made her knees buckle. His tongue was a hot invader in her mouth, possessive, taking, sweeping across every surface. Every nerve fired, cream soaked her thong, and every pulse point in her body pounded with need.

When he finally lifted his mouth from hers, she had to cling to his wrists to steady herself. The look in his eyes undid her. It was so ravenous and possessive that her breath caught in her throat.

"I think it's time for something else to be in that sweet mouth," he told her. "Take off your clothes."

Still trembling, she stripped as quickly as she

could. Then she dropped to her knees in front of him, awaiting his next command.

He pulled his T-shirt over his head and tossed it aside.

"Do you know that D/s is not always all about pain, girl?"

"Yes, Master. It's about submitting to the will of your Dom. Trusting him to always take care of you. Giving him the power to use you as he wishes because in doing so you serve his pleasure."

"Very good." He rid himself of his boots, jeans, and boxer briefs.

Her eyes widened as she caught sight of his cock, long, thick, and swollen, the head a deep red. The walls of her pussy clenched in response to the sight. God, how she wanted him inside her.

"I promise you, I will never abuse that privilege." He glanced at the cards. "The whip? The paddle? Even the heavy nipple clamps we used the other night? They all give us both extreme pleasure. But right now, I want to do something I haven't done in a long time."

"And what's that, Master?"

"I want to fuck you so hard that when you come, you'll scream my name. I want that connection with you. We have to have it for this to work."

Oh, god!

They had tumbled deep into this very fast, but she was glad of it. She wanted this, too. She wanted to be sure that what she'd felt from the first moment was real.

"Then please do that, Master."

"Tell me what you want," he insisted.

She chewed her lower lip. He had asked her what her desire was and expected her to be truthful with him.

She discovered she wasn't afraid to tell him. "I want you to fuck me. I want your cock inside me. I want you to fuck me until I lose my mind."

The smile he gave her was both ravenous and self-satisfied. "Rise, sub."

She got shakily to her feet.

"Don't move," he commanded.

Fee didn't think she could, even if she wanted to. She watched as Cade rummaged through a dresser drawer and pulled out a bright red ball gag and a condom. He rolled the latex onto his enormous cock then picked up the gag.

"We don't want any of the ranch hands rushing up here thinking I'm murdering someone." He deftly fitted the gag into her mouth and buckled its straps behind her head. "On the bed on hands and knees," he ordered. "Place yourself at the edge so I can stand behind you."

When she was in position, he moved into place behind her. Two of his fingers slipped into her, testing her readiness. Was he shocked at how drenched she was already?

"Hot and wet, and instantly ready for me." His voice was hoarse. "Excellent. That's what I want. So I can fuck you any time the urge hits me. You're tight, but you can take me." He leaned down and nipped her shoulder. "And then I will own you, girl. Do you understand?"

She nodded, unable to speak, but a tiny thrill wriggled through her.

"Good."

He pressed the head of his shaft at her opening, gripped her hips with his hands, and slowly eased himself inside her, one thick inch at a time.

"Breathe," he ordered. "Take deep breaths. It will make it easier. Get ready, girl, because I want this right now."

She was glad he'd buckled the gag into her mouth because as he thrust in and out of her, pounding her, punctuating some of his thrusts with hard slaps to her ass, the pleasure coursed through her like a hot river. As he drove into her harder and harder, the spankings increased until the pleasurable pain filled every space and crevice and she lost a sense of anything except the sensations and the feel of his cock.

She was so close to the edge. Tears from the effort to hold back until he gave the command gathered in her eyes and rolled down her cheeks. And still he plunged on and on.

She was barely aware of his fingers digging into her hips again or his balls slapping into her inner thighs.

"Now." He gave a hoarse shout. "Now, girl. Come with me now."

She exploded as he pumped into her, and his cock pulsed again and again. Her body shook so hard she thought her bones rattled. The orgasm gripped her in a tight fist and shook her, tumbling her through space until at last —at last!—the spasms began to subside. She fell forward on the bed, her arms too weak to hold her any longer. Her ass was still on fire, her face soaked with tears, and she had never felt so satisfied, so complete in her entire life.

Cade eased himself from her body, and she heard him dispose of the condom. Then he lifted her in his arms and lay down on the bed with her, pulling her against his body. She could feel the heavy beat of his heart against her back.

"That was very good, girl." His voice still had a rough sound to it. "Better than good." He turned her in his arms so he could see her face, fingers brushing at the tears on her cheeks. "I want you, Fee."

Her eyes widened at his use of her name.

"Yes," he acknowledged, knowing what she was asking. "I used your name, so there won't be any mistaking who is with me. Who I *know* is with me. Clint was right, damn him. You're exactly what I needed. Need," he corrected.

"He was right about me, too." She sighed, pleasurable warmth coursing through her. "If it's Dealer's Choice, I choose you."

"Good." He gave her a soft kiss. "We'll set our own rules this weekend and see how it goes. But make no mistake. I don't intend to let you get away."

"Does that mean you get to be the dealer now?"

"When I choose. Sometimes, though, I'll want you to deal the cards. We'll have a long time to get that right. Does that work for you?"

"Yes, Master." She grinned. "Yes, Cade. It works just fine."

And it did.

Two of a Kind

Risa Channing tipped the cab driver, gathered her leather coat around her, and pressed the brass knocker on the heavy, carved wooden door. She did her best to tamp down a sudden flutter of nerves as the door to Rawhide swung open. She stepped into the warm, paneled reception area and tentatively smiled at the man standing there.

"Hello, Clint."

She had met Clint Chavez, the club's owner, when she filled out her membership application and he took her on a tour of the dungeon.

"Welcome, Risa. We're so pleased you've decided to join us."

Risa nodded, hoping she'd be just as happy by the end of the evening. Unsatisfied for a long time with the Doms she'd played with—and the ones she'd had unfortunate relationships with—she hoped that she'd find here what she was looking for. More than that. What she'd craved.

When she'd met with Ruelas, the mysterious Dungeon Master of Rawhide, she'd been very emphatic that she wanted a session with an experienced Dom who could take her to the next level of BDSM. She'd wanted such an experience for a long time, but until recently, hadn't had the nerve to go through with it. What if she hated it? Regretted it? Couldn't play beyond the light level she was used to?

Too late now, kiddo.

The only thing Clint had told her was the man was a SEAL on leave, with a permanent guest pass. And he was so sought after that when word got out he might visit, subs lined up for a session with him.

"Ruelas is waiting for you in the lounge," Clint told her, taking Risa's coat and purse. They'd be put in a locker for her until she was ready to leave. "Have a good evening."

I hope so.

"Thank you."

Risa smoothed the short skirt and halter-top. She'd left her hair down tonight, swinging just below her shoulders. Beneath the skirt, she wore a brand-new scarlet thong. For luck.

As she entered the lounge, she saw Ruelas sitting on a curved section of a couch. Although he was of medium height, he carried himself in a way as to seem much taller. He wore his blond hair in a long tail and was dressed in his signature navy silk shirt and pants. He spotted her and stood, his hand extended, a smile on his face.

"Good evening, Risa." He lifted her hand and kissed her knuckles. "We've been waiting for you."

The man sitting next to him rose, and immediately, Risa felt her thong dampen even as her mouth went dry.

Like Ruelas, he appeared taller than he was, his shoulders broad and his chest and abs hard and flat, with a sexy dusting of dark hair. All the rippling muscles were easy to see because he was bare from the waist up. The rest of his body was clad in leather pants, tight enough to reveal the thick bulge of his cock.

Below that, he was barefoot. She noticed his feet appeared as graceful as the rest of his body.

But it was his face that caught her attention. Framed by a thick fall of inky black hair, it was a warrior's face, finely chiseled with a square jaw, and startling blue eyes that looked out from thick lashes. The power he exuded was so strong as to be nearly visible in the air around him. She could only stand there mesmerized and so aroused she needed every bit of discipline to keep herself together.

She wasn't looking for more than one night of intense pleasure. Was she?

"Risa." Ruelas' voice penetrated the fog wrapped around her brain. "This is Master J."

Her eyes drank him in as they kept returning to the significant bulge in his pants. She could hardly wait to feel that inside her. At his pleasure, of course.

Master J, in full Dom mode, did not extend his hand. Instead, he let his gaze travel slowly over her. She could feel his eyes undressing her in a way that she might as well have been naked.

He nodded at Ruelas. "She will do very nicely."

Ruelas smiled. "You know it is always my goal to please." He looked at Risa. "I have passed along your desires to Master J, and I assure you he can more than satisfy them. Beyond that, Risa, you can trust him completely."

Her mouth was so dry she had to swallow before she could speak. Every nerve in her body vibrated, and her pulse throbbed in her core.

"Thank you, Ruelas." She lowered her eyes. "And thank you, Master J."

"The room is prepared for you," the Dungeon

Master told the Dom. "Everything is as you requested."

"Good. Then we shouldn't waste any more time."

Okay, so no small talk or let's get acquainted.

Well, this was what she'd asked for, right? A complete Dom who would take her well into the next level of BDSM play. Someone who could satisfy the very dark desires that claimed her dreams and left her shaken when she awoke, more often than not, with her hand still on her clit. At first, she'd been embarrassed to admit to herself that pain was a great aphrodisiac. But when she squeezed her nipples or her hard clit, cream gushed from her and her pussy flexed with spasms.

She'd tried to figure out a way to spank herself, but the position was too awkward to do any good, so she had to be contented with reading about it. Caning particularly appealed to her. The book she'd ordered online came with explicit photographs of women after they'd been caned, and she ached for her ass to burn like theirs. To have hot stripes that made it difficult for her to sit anywhere. Whatever surface she chose would press against the residual soreness, so the sweet pain would be with her wherever she went.

She'd spent weeks agonizing over the decision and then decided to apply for membership at Rawhide—a new environment for her and one that had by far the best reputation in the area as far as clientele went. She certainly hoped so, since the membership fee was steep.

But in clubs where she'd previously belonged or visited, none of the Doms had impressed her enough with his skills to take her to the next level. Plus, with a new level of play, she wanted a new environment. Someplace where her old self wasn't present and where she could explore new horizons freely.

"Girl." Master J's deep voice was like a hot caress.

"Yes, Sir."

"Follow me. Our evening is about to begin."

The room he led her into looked much the same as others she'd been in, only more elaborate and luxurious. As Master J locked the door and adjusted the lighting, she took the opportunity to glance around.

The floor was covered with a thick carpet except for one large square of polished hardwood. Risa expected that was for subs who needed to be punished in a kneeling position. No soft cushioning for them. The room also contained a padded spanking bench, manacles hanging from the ceiling with matching cuffs at floor level, a St. Andrews Cross, a cupboard open to display a number of toys and instruments, and something she had only seen pictures of—an old-fashioned pillory.

The punishment equipment of years gone by.

The original ones had places for the head and hands to rest and hinged boards to keep them in place. The ones she'd read about, like this one, also had a place for a woman's breasts to be contained. A fresh spate of cream soaked her thong as she imagined the things that could be done to a woman held helpless in the apparatus.

A small table with two chairs sat at the side. The only thing on its surface was a deck of cards. Risa looked at him, wondering if it was okay to ask about them.

She waited for instructions while Master J slowly walked around her. She could sense the impact of his gaze on her as he studied her from every angle.

"Before we begin, Ruelas gave me the specifics of

your request," he told her. "Look at me, Risa." His voice was softer now.

She raised her eyes, questioning. "Yes, Master J?"

"Ruelas takes his requests very seriously. He wants to make sure that those he pairs together are a suitable match." He brushed a stray strand of hair back from her face. "For what we are about to do—especially to take you to levels you've never reached before—there must be complete and absolute trust. I promise you that you have nothing to fear from me. You can trust me to not only satisfy your desires and stretch your limits but to not push you beyond them if it becomes too much for you. Do you understand?"

She nodded.

He picked up the deck of cards sitting in front of him. "Cut the cards."

She stared at him, confused.

"Did you not understand? It's a simple request. If you didn't understand that, then…"

Swallowing, she cut the deck.

"Very good. I am going to deal some cards. I want you to tell me exactly what it is you're seeking tonight. I want to hear it from you, one desire for each card."

He slid the top card off the deck and turned it over. The King of Spades.

How appropriate. "I have discovered that I want to explore greater levels of pain," she told him. "I want you to rule over me and help me reach that point where the pain itself is a pleasure."

He turned over the next card. The Jack of Spades.

"To be helpless, except to do as you command me."

The Queen of Diamonds.

"Aah." She exhaled, watching his reaction. "To achieve the intense orgasms possible at that level. I-I've discovered that pain increases my pleasure, that it takes me to a place where things could be ever too much."

Another card. The Ace of Spades. Of course.

"I want to reach the highest level of pain I can endure, one that gives you pleasure as intense as mine."

His lips twitched as if he was holding back a smile. His gaze softened, but there was still hunger flaring in his dilated irises.

Risa's breath caught as the heat of his gaze seared her, sending shivers skating over her skin. She'd only wanted this one night, but suddenly, she wanted much more than that. From him. With him. And the intensity of her need frightened her. She'd spent her entire life being careful not to let her emotions rule her mind, so how had this even happened?

"I have been a Dom for many years, Risa. I like to think I have pleased my subs, given them what they wanted, and that I did it well. That is the reason Ruelas selected me for this evening. I will never, ever take a sub to a point where it would be emotionally harmful. Give me your trust, Risa, and I will give you what you need. So I ask you now, are you ready for this evening?"

"Yes, Master."

"Then before we begin, I must have your safeword."

She had always used *stoplight*, figuring the significance of the word itself would help convey her meaning. But for tonight, she'd chosen something else.

"Nightbird."

Tonight, she expected to fly.

Master J. tilted up her face with one finger beneath her chin. Something like humor momentarily flashed in his eyes.

"Then I will make sure you fly tonight." He released her chin. "You know the rules. You will address me as Master or Master J. You may not ask questions unless I give you permission. You will speak only when spoken to except to use your safeword, which you will use only when you are certain you want me to stop. And you will obey my every command. Understood?"

"Yes, Master J." His name sensuously rolled off her tongue.

Apparently satisfied with the atmosphere in the room, Master J took up a position in the center of the floor, legs apart, arms folded across his chest.

"Submissive pose, girl," he ordered.

Risa obediently dropped to her knees before him, eyes downcast, head bowed, hands behind her back.

"Excellent. Rise and remove your clothing, everything except your shoes."

Risa rose to her feet. Still keeping her gaze on the floor, she unfastened the halter top and dropped it beside her. Trembling with anticipation, she slid down the zipper on her micro skirt, stepped out of it, and let it fall on top of the halter. She hooked her thumbs into the thin elastic straps holding the thong in place and eased it down her legs, awkwardly balancing herself on her stiletto heels as she stepped out of it. But when she would have added it to the other items, Master J took it from her hands and pressed it to his face.

Closing his eyes, he inhaled. "Exquisite. And so wet. I'm pleased that you are already so aroused."

Risa just stood there, hands behind her back, thrilled that her scent pleased him.

"Turn around," he commanded. "Slowly. I want to see every inch of you."

She had only moved partway around when he clasped a hand around her arm and stopped her.

"Submissive pose."

Immediately, she sank to her knees, unease fluttering in her stomach. Had she done something to displease him already? What could it be? Would he decide to end the session?

Holding her breath, she waited for his next order.

"Touch your forehead to the floor, knees wide apart. Yes, like that. Now reach behind you and separate the cheeks of your ass. I want to see every bit of you exposed." There was as much possessiveness in his tone as there was domination. Something was definitely happening between them.

If possible, she felt even more naked, aware that he could see every inch of her pussy and her ass. A whisper of sound told her he'd moved up behind her. In a moment, one finger touched her, sliding slowly from her clit, down the length of her pussy, stopping at her opening to probe lightly inside before finally rimming her anus. A shiver of delight skated over her skin.

"Such an enticing cunt," he murmured. "And a delicious ass. Tonight, I'll make sure to work both of them properly."

She heard him step away.

"On your feet, girl, and walk over to the pillory and place yourself properly. It's one of my favorite instruments and a good way to begin our evening."

Risa slightly shook as she walked over to the

apparatus and pressed against it. Resting her chin in the curve for her head, she placed her hands and her breasts where Master J indicated and waited for him to lock her into it. The wood was polished and smooth against her skin, obviously sanded to prevent splinters from harming a sub.

As he latched each section into place, the realization that she was now completely helpless excited her beyond belief. He could do whatever he chose to her, and she was powerless to stop him. The throbbing in her cunt accelerated, vibrating through her body.

"It excites me to have my sub so restrained," he said as he adjusted all the hinged bars. "It leaves you totally at my mercy." He paused. "Does that excite you?"

"Yes, Master J. It does." More than she'd ever expected. Until now, she'd only had either her wrists or her ankles manacled, never both at the same time. And never in a position of such complete helplessness, with no movement allowed at all and her entire body exposed to whatever her Dom chose to do.

Yet she had no hesitation about this with Master J. The pulse in her cunt throbbed harder, and cream trickled to the inside of her thighs.

Silently, he locked the head restraints in place, then the wrists, and finally the breasts. Except for her feet, she was completely immobilized. And she had never been so aroused in her life. The tiny edge of fear, of the unknown, only served to ramp up her arousal.

Master J walked around to stand in front of her, a tiny smile of satisfaction curving his lips. His mouth fascinated her, and she wondered how it would feel on her nipples and her clit. She had to bite down on her lip to control the excitement rushing through her.

"Afraid already?" Master J asked.

"No, Master." She swiped her tongue across her lower lip. "May I say, instead, that I am eager to experience what awaits me?"

Heat flamed in his eyes. "I'll do my best to live up to your expectations."

Moving closer, he squeezed her constricted breasts, kneading them before taking each nipple between thumb and forefinger and squeezing them. Tiny sparks of erotic pain shot though her breasts and spread down to her cunt. He knew how to apply just the right amount of pressure to give her the most pleasure.

"Look at me," Master J commanded. "Let me see your eyes. Good. I can see the pleasure in them. You enjoy pain. But you'll tell me when it gets past that edge of sweetness."

Risa gritted her teeth at the first edge of pain. But as the intensity increased, she welcomed it. Pain had always been a great stimulant. For whatever reason, it stimulated her pheromones and put her in a state of sexual need. Even pain that occurred outside the bedroom, which could sometimes make for an embarrassing situation. This was the major reason why she'd wanted to experiment with higher levels.

Master J continued to pinch and twist until her pebbled tips were swollen and pleasantly aching. He bent his head and licked each nipple, then lightly bit each one before walking around to her back. She squeezed her thighs together, trying to control the tremors in her pussy.

The next sensation was his hand trailing down her

spine to her ass, cupping each cheek before probing the hot crevice between her globes. She clenched at his touch, trying to trap his hand, but he laughed, a low, rough sound that left her swallowing hard.

"Not yet, girl. Not just yet."

She was totally unprepared for the slap on her buttocks, the hard contact of flesh on flesh, and she jerked. But Master J gave that warm-as-molasses laugh and lightly pinched her. Then his lips were at her ear, his breath a faint breeze against her skin.

"I need to warm up that sweet ass of yours before we move on to the good stuff."

Smack!

His hard hand landed again, and the pain began to spread over her entire buttocks and down to her thighs. A pleasurable heat made her body silently beg for more. She wished she could ask him to keep his hand on her just for a moment after the contact, so she could feel his fingers' warmth through the searing heat the slap created.

This time, she only slightly jerked. She even saucily wiggled her rear end at him.

The next blow was sharper, harder, and then they came in rapid, but uneven, succession. She had no way to anticipate when the next one would fall, which only made her more excited. The heat and pain continued to spread in waves of bliss.

When he stopped, she wanted to cry out in protest, but she swallowed the words. Nothing happened for a long moment, and she wondered if he'd stopped for good. Had her reaction in some way displeased him? Did he want her to cry out more, to beg him to stop? Her stomach knotted with tension.

He was in front of her again. With her head locked in the position it was in, she couldn't keep it submissively lowered, so she clearly saw him. Desire still flared in his eyes, and the muscles in his jaw tightened. She had never met a man who aroused her so instantly or to such heights. Or who called to something dark inside her the way Master J did.

She was so ready for whatever he wanted. It wasn't just his knowledgeable touch or his expertise at administering pain. He knew what to do and exactly how to do it. It was more than that. The man himself gave off such sensual vibes she could feel them surrounding her with every breath.

His lips curved in a tiny smile as his gaze locked with hers. He held a crop in his hand, one that had a short but thin tail, like a miniature whip. He kept drawing it slowly across his palm.

"Has anyone ever used this on your breasts, girl?"

His voice was so mesmerizing she almost forgot to answer him.

"Uh, no. I mean, no Master J."

"But you'd like that, yes?"

She wet her lips. "Yes. Master."

As long as it's you.

And where had *that* thought come from?

"We'll begin with some light strokes. This is something you must get used to."

He trailed the thin strip of leather back and forth across her breasts until she was ready to beg for him to get on with it. That was the moment he chose to give the crop a hard flick of his wrist, and it stroked across both breasts, drawing a soft line of pain across her skin.

Master J watched her carefully as he applied the

little whip again and again. The strokes were never hard, but each one had a bite. And each took her breath away, not from the pain, but from the eroticism of the sharp sting on her tender flesh. Her breasts quivered in response, and her nipples hardened to stiff peaks. Even this quickly, she could sense her orgasm begin to gather low in her body.

Master J cupped her jaw and looked directly into her eyes.

"You find that stimulating. Good. Suspected you would. And we have barely begun." He drew his tongue lightly along her lips, her body trembling in response. "But remember. You will not come until I give you permission. Do you know what happens to bad girls who do that?"

She shook her head within its limited motion.

"I arouse them in ways they never imagined, then leave them tied in such a way that they cannot even bring themselves to orgasm. So you'll follow the rules."

I'll do my best.

He moved away, and when he returned behind her, she sensed the long, round smoothness of what had to be a cane.

"Ruelas said that caning was on your wish list." He brought his head close to hers and gently nipped the tender skin where her neck and shoulder met. "I'm an expert at this. It's one of my favorite edge-play activities."

He trailed his mouth across her nape and nibbled at the other shoulder. "I use a thin cane because it produces a sharper, more pleasurable pain. Each one builds on the previous stroke, giving you the sensation of a burn. You will feel it on your ass, your thighs, even your cunt." He drew his tongue along her spine. "Since this is your first time, I'll only give you ten strokes tonight. Then, you'll tell me how it made you feel."

She drew in a deep breath, let it out slowly, and closed her eyes. She didn't know which was exciting her more, the anticipation of the cane or Master J's mouth on her body. She prayed he would use both on her more. That and any other instruments that he chose.

Beyond the pain and realization of her sexual fantasies, something electrically charged kept zinging between them. While she had desired a lot of men, once they were finished with playtime, she never thought of them until she was ready to play again. Master J had such an intense, emotional impact on her from the moment she'd seen him that she was unsure how to deal with it.

And unless she was mistaken, the same feelings had wrapped themselves around him.

Risa was so busy letting her mind wildly race over this idea that she forgot to brace herself for the first blow. It fell, sharp and stinging, across her buttock. She bit down on her lip to keep from crying out. The next one fell without warning, and after that, they hit sporadically, heat spreading from the cheeks of her ass down to her thighs and her pussy. As each cry tried to force itself from her mouth, she swallowed it back. But by the third or fourth blow, the edge of pain had been dulled by the intense pleasure rushing through her. She couldn't help the little moan that escaped her.

Master J was running the palm of his hand over her again, smoothing her burning flesh. She was stunned when he placed a kiss on each globe of her buttocks. "You have a very sweet ass, girl. I can't wait to fuck it."

And I can't wait to have you do it.

She wanted to come badly. Her thighs were sticky with her cream, and her pussy throbbed with hunger. She wanted to beg him for permission, yet at the same time, she wanted him to know he had all the control.

Master J's fingers traced the line of her slit, and he hummed with satisfaction. "I think it wouldn't take much to push you into that orgasm you so badly want," he said. "And you'll have it, but only when I'm ready to allow you."

"Thank you, Master J."

As she waited for whatever came next, Risa was suddenly aware that whatever was happening Master J felt the intensity, too.

What the hell?

She hadn't come here looking for anything beyond one night of extreme satisfaction. Of exploring new boundaries. Her other attempts to connect emotionally with a Dom had exploded and left her badly burned. Besides, how could she develop feelings for someone this fast when she'd spent so much time separating herself from her everyday life and the Doms she played with? She knew she had to fight this—whatever *this* was—but she seemed to have little control of the emotion surging through her, squeezing her heart and warming her from the inside out.

"When we're finished, I'll put some special cream on you to ease any discomfort." He gave a slight groan. "I wish you could see how beautiful your ass is with these red stripes on it. I'd love to run my tongue over each one. And maybe I will before our session is over." He gave her buttocks a soft slap. "Spread your feet wider, girl. I have a treat for you."

She widened her stance as much as she could. She didn't know which was making her more uncomfortable, the residual soreness from the spanking, the whipping and caning, or the position in the pillory. She felt herself falling away from the pain into subspace, where she was disconnected from everything except sensation and her Master could do anything at all. She trusted Ruelas to have matched her with a trustworthy Dom. And besides, whatever that feeling was that was building inside her, she was assured that she was truly safe with him.

She closed her eyes for a moment, centering herself, and was shocked to feel Master J's lips on hers. Doms usually avoided kissing because it was too personal. His mouth was firm and smooth, and he exerted just the right pressure. The tip of his tongue traced the seam of her lips, a tiny flame searing her mouth. Her eyes flew open, and she found him staring into them.

"Open your mouth, girl," he ordered.

When she did, his tongue thrust inside and licked every inner inch, dueling with her tongue, sending some kind of message she was desperately trying to interpret. When he lifted his head, she experienced a quick sense of loss. But he held out his hands, and she saw a gleaming pair of nipple clips. Her heartbeat quickened again.

****

Risa Channing was delicious. That was the only word Jax Schroyer could think of to describe her. The minute he'd met her, he knew he was in trouble. Based on her request, he'd expected a sub with a hard edge, submissive yet always wanting more. Edgier.

He couldn't have been more off base. Ruelas had said she would prove to be an excellent sub. That she had come recommended and that he'd find her pleasing. Pleasing, for God's sake!

That was kind of like saying a pussy was wet.

And speaking of wet, Risa was a walking wet dream. He guessed her height at five-foot-four, but the sexy stiletto heels added another three inches. Lustrous auburn hair fell in waves to her shoulders and was matched by the narrow strip of carefully trimmed curls at the lips of her cunt. Her ass, sweetly striped with the marks of the cane, curved gently down to her thighs, and he wanted to sink his fingers into it. Her breasts, while not large, were still full and tipped with dusky nipples. She certainly looked good enough to eat, immobilized in the pillory. He wanted to run his tongue all over her and take her home with him.

Take her home? Wait just a minute here.

Jax was a loner, had been for years. He'd discovered the hard way that his needs as a Dom didn't appeal to too many subs. The ones who enjoyed the extreme play he wanted weren't anyone he wanted to spend more than a few hours with. Ever.

So what was it about this woman who had grabbed him from the moment he'd set eyes on her? Was it the faint air of vulnerability combined with an inner strength? Was it her willingness to explore more extreme planes of BDSM without either the sharp edge or excessive attitude of submission he'd found in other subs?

Maybe it was all of them, but something about her had unlocked the emotional door he'd kept secure for most of his adult life. Whatever it was, he'd better get her out of his mind. She'd asked for one night, and for this night, he was going to take her for the ride of her life. And that was it. He'd been down this road before and still had the scars to prove it. He'd just have to get his rebellious emotions under control.

Spanking and caning her had aroused him so much he had a slight difficulty walking. Now, he was going to move her on to something else, and he wondered how long it would be before he gave in to his own desires and shoved his cock into her cunt or her mouth.

Or her ass.

Her eyes widened at the clothespins he'd held up at her eye level. He watched for signs of fear but saw only desire, need, and excitement.

Again, his traitorous emotions were jumping all over the place. Here was a woman who obviously had great depths and who enjoyed the extremes of BDSM as he did. Could he take a chance here? All through the session, his gut had been twisted into a knot as he battled the thought. He'd followed that road before with disastrous results. He'd promised himself never to do it again. To take his pleasure where he found it and that was all.

He deliberately swept everything out of his mind to concentrate on the play at hand.

"Have your other Doms decorated your nipples or compressed them in any way?" he asked.

She shook her head.

"Words, girl," Jax reminded her.

"No, Sir, they have not."

"For needing to be reminded to answer properly, I think one or two more strikes with the cane are in order."

He picked up the cane from where he'd left it and applied it twice with increased force across her reddened skin. When he moved around to look at her face again, her eyes were glazed. The look he'd seen with subs who got high on pain. Who fell into subspace as the pain increased with every touch and tempo across their flesh.

She'd certainly been truthful. This was what she craved.

He bent slightly and took her nipples in his mouth, each in turn, tugging with his lips and gently biting. They tasted so sweet he was sure he could spend hours doing this to them and never tire of it. Her soft, little moans excited him. He bit a little harder before lifting his head. Then he picked up the clothespins again.

"I use these rather than jewelry," he told her. "I see jewelry as a more personal item, a gift between a Dom and sub in a relationship. Plus, the clothespins work much better at compressing the entire nipple. Like this."

Jax took one nipple between thumb and forefinger and pinched the pebbled surface hard. She sucked in a breath, but her eyes, still slightly glazed, never left his face. Releasing the bud, he placed one pin on it, making sure the entire surface was contained. The tiny whimper that escaped her mouth was definitely one of pleasure rather than protest. When he did the same with the other nipple, she hummed with ecstasy.

But the real test would come with the next move.

"I'm going to touch your clit, girl. As aroused as you are, it will make you want to come. But I order you not to. If you do, I'll need to punish you again." He couldn't help smiling at the way a hint of a grin played on her lips. "And no fair deliberately disobeying me."

He squatted down in front of her and pushed her legs even farther apart. When he ran his fingers along her slit, he discovered she was even more drenched than before. Just the ghost of a touch on her clit made her quiver with restrained need. He was tempted to leave her like this, lightly toying with her clit yet denying her the opportunity to come. But that would be for another time. If there *was* another time, which he was fervently beginning to hope there would be.

He lightly tugged on the swollen nub, made sure it was well-coated with her juices. She gasped slightly at the pinch of wood on her sensitive flesh, but then he could almost sense her settle herself. When he was satisfied with his work, he rose to his feet and cupped her cheeks.

"All right?" he asked.

Although she had drifted into subspace, heat and hunger still danced in her eyes. And something else. Something evident in every submissive line of her body. Every reaction. It was admiration for him as a Dom. It shocked him that she would react that way in such a short time and made him wonder at the ineptness of her former Doms.

"Yes, Master J. Very much so." Her voice had a breathy quality to it, evidence of her arousal and the effort it was taking to keep herself under control, even with the pain and discomfort she had to be feeling from the unnatural position in the pillory.

"Excellent." Jax couldn't help brushing his lips against her, tasting the sweetness.

She reached something inside him that no other sub had ever touched. He sensed no artifice in her, nothing fake, and nothing hard or worn. She was a beautiful sub inside and out, and the Dom she chose would be a very special person to her. Something he'd never had with the other women he'd known. He didn't know whether to be angry about it or embrace it.

Shaking off the turmoil racing around in his mind, he opened a drawer in the tall cupboard against the wall, studied the contents, and removed two dildos, one slightly thicker than the other. After picking up a tube of lubricant, he crossed back to Risa.

"How are your nipples, girl? And your clit? Can you feel the pressure from the clothespins?"

"Yes, Master." She swiped her tongue across her lower lip. "Thank you for fastening them on me."

Better and better. Jax swallowed a smile. "Very good."

Standing behind her, he spread the cheeks of her ass with one hand, pressed the tip of the tube of lubricant to her anus and gently squeezed. When he was satisfied he'd applied a sufficient amount, he shifted the tube to the other hand and slowly inserted two fingers of the other into her hole. She was hot and tight, her muscles clenching around him. He added a third finger, stretching her tissues until he was sure he'd prepared her properly. Then, without giving her any warning, he took the thickest of the dildos and pressed it inside her ass with a steady stroke.

"Ahhhhh."

The sound came from deep within her, and her entire body tightened.

"Easy," he crooned. "We're only halfway there."

Standing in front of her again, he took a moment to admire her locked into a completely helpless position, the clothespins on her nipples and clit only adding to her discomfort. Yet, there was no mistaking the pleasure on her face.

"One more little toy," he told her. "Open your mouth, girl. I'm going to pretend this is my cock in there, because my real cock will be busy elsewhere."

She obediently opened as wide as she could, and Jax slid the dildo onto her tongue and into her mouth as far as it would go. With her head immobilized, there was limited maneuverability, but she managed to take a good bit of it. Only then did he step back and remove his leather pants, easing them down over his thick, swollen cock.

He was grateful to see her eyes widen in both amazement and approval, but he took only a moment to enjoy it. Carefully, he unlocked her from the pillory, head first, then her hands, and finally her breasts. She'd need good aftercare, but now wasn't the moment to think about that. The discomfort from being locked into position for so long would increase her arousal.

Taking care not to dislodge either of the dildos, he arranged Risa on the floor so she was balanced on her hands and knees, and he knelt behind her.

"Arms crossed in front of you," he commanded, "and head resting on them. Now, girl."

He took a moment to study her in the vulnerable position. He was doing his best to keep his barriers in place, to remind himself that this was one night and he'd walk away from it. By choice. Nothing good could come of taking it beyond this.

But looking at her made his heart twist. Made him want things he'd sworn never to reach for. And once he penetrated her with his shaft, the ultimate bonding, he'd be working damned hard to keep that vow in place.

Just remember. Once and done and you don't get burned.

As soon as she'd positioned herself, Jax rolled on a condom and drove into her with one hard thrust. She was so liquid, the glide was an easy one, but once inside her, he had to stop and catch his breath.

To him, all these years, a pussy was just a pussy. As many subs as he'd fucked, he'd achieved varying degrees of physical satisfaction. But this? This was an entirely new experience. If he didn't think he was losing his mind, he'd say it was as much emotional as it was physical.

If he was given to fancy words and phrases, he'd say having his cock in Risa's cunt was an almost mystical experience. How the hell had this happened?

Forget it, asshole. Been there done that, got the bruises to prove it, right?

Not right, but right now, every nerve in his body was focused on his cock and the woman it was buried inside. Bending over her so he could reach her breasts and squeeze them, adding to the pressure of the clothespins, he pumped in and out of her tight muscles, back and forth, and she matched his rhythm. The dildo in her ass made it such a tight fit, her flesh scraping against his with every stroke. His balls tightened, and his release came roaring up from deep inside him.

"Now," he hoarsely shouted. "Come now, girl."

She bore down on him, her core tightening like a steel fist, squeezing as her body shuddered again and again. Reaching between her thighs, he tugged on the clothespin on her clit, prolonging her orgasm until she collapsed forward, his cock still inside her, clothespins still attached, dildo still in her ass.

He softly smoothed his hands over her until the last of her aftershocks subsided. Then he carefully withdrew and set about removing all the toys. He rose, disposed of the condom, then lifted her in his arms and carried her to a padded table covered with a soft cotton cloth.

"Rest easy now," he crooned in a low voice. "Let me take care of you."

He rubbed and massaged all her muscles, especially the ones strained from her position in the pillory. Then he bathed her with a warm cloth and finally applied soothing ointments, being extra liberal on her reddened ass.

Aftercare had always been important to him. He despised Doms who used their subs, causing them pain and then leaving them to their own devices to tend to their aching skin and muscles. He felt it both a responsibility and an obligation and always made it part of the scene.

"You'll have some problems sitting this week," he told her with a rueful grin.

She smiled, and something turned over inside him. "It was worth it. Can I ask you something?" Her voice had a hesitant sound to it.

"Sure. I can't promise I'll answer it."

"It doesn't require an answer, just an action. Would you kiss me? Sort of like you did before?"

Would he? Jax ground his teeth. He was afraid if he did that, he'd lose the barrier he'd tried so hard to keep between them tonight. But lord knew he wanted to in the worst way.

"I know kissing usually isn't a part of this, but could I have just one? I want to taste your mouth again."

What the hell? Maybe it would help him get her out of his mind after tonight.

He should have just bent down and kissed her where she lay on the table. Idiot that he was, he picked her up in his arms and carried her to the big leather chair in one corner.

He sat down with her on his lap. Threading his fingers through her hair and clasping her head, he lowered his mouth to hers, ran his tongue along the seam of her lips, and when she opened for him, he thrust inside.

Holy sweet Jesus!

She was every good thing he'd ever tasted in his life. Alarm bells were clanging in his head, but they were drowned out by the thudding of his heart. Her small tongue danced with his, playing with it. Heat surged through him, a funny feeling swirled in his stomach, and he never wanted to let her go.

So now what?

****

Risa had to hold on tight to Master J to keep from falling off his lap as he kissed her. Her head was swimming, and every nerve in her body was doing a happy dance. She'd just thought the kiss would be…nice. Hot. A reminder of tonight and maybe something to entice him to play again.

But holy shit!

His lips were warm and firm, his tongue like a flame in her mouth, a surge of heat that raced straight to her nipples and her pussy. And worst of all, to her heart.

No, no, no! Don't be stupid. Not again.

Her brain seemed to have dropped into cold

storage. She wanted this man and not just for this moment.

When they broke the kiss, breathless, they stared at each other. The same stunned expression on his face mirrored what she was sure was on her own. For a very long moment, neither of them moved.

"Well," she said at last.

"Well, indeed." His gaze was still locked with hers.

Then they spoke at the same time.

"I don't want you to think—"

"I need to explain—"

Risa touched her fingertips to his mouth. "Me, first. Whatever this is turning out to be, it's on me, and I don't expect a thing from you."

He gave a hoarse laugh. "Funny, I was just about to say the same thing."

Again, they stared at each other.

She cleared her throat. "I haven't had a lot of luck taking things outside the playroom."

"Neither have I." He feathered a brief kiss over her lips. "Maybe we should try this one more time and see what happens."

"I—I'd like that."

His gaze was still glued to her face. "How about my booking a room for an overnight? We can see where it goes from there."

"That would be very nice." Risa smiled. "Master J."

"Actually, it's Jax. Jax Schroyer."

"Nice to meet you, Jax Schroyer."

"Same goes, Risa Channing. The same definitely goes."

About the Author

USA Today Bestselling and Award-winning author Desiree Holt writes everything from romantic suspense and paranormal to erotic, and has been referred to by *USA Today* as the Nora Roberts of erotic romance. She is a winner of the EPIC E-Book Award, the Holt Medallion, and a Romantic Times Reviewers Choice nominee. She has been featured on *CBS Sunday Morning* and in *The Village Voice, The Daily Beast, USA Today, The (London) Daily Mail, The New Delhi Times,* and numerous other national and international publications.

~*~

Visit Desiree at
www.DesireeHolt.com
www.desireesplace.net
www.facebook.com/desireeholtauthor
www.facebook.com/desiree01holt
Twitter @desireeholt
Pinterest: desiree02holt
Follow me on BookBub
https://www.bookbub.com/search?search=Desiree+Holt

Sign up for her newsletter and receive a free book:
https://desireeholt.com/newsletter/

Rawhide: Volume One
By Desiree Holt

Crack the Whip

Rancher Reece Halliday is shocked to learn the new manager of his fetish club, Rawhide, is Katie Warren, the woman he loved and lost due to his sexual preferences. But time has passed and Katie has discovered the lure and satisfaction of BDSM—including the pleasurable sting of a single tail whip. Can Reece lure her back into his arms—and bed—when he cracks the whip during their private sessions?

Slapping Leather

Liz Gillibrand needs a man she can submit to while keeping her sex life a secret from the conservative ranching community. Been there. Done that. Ended badly. But the first Dom she sees at Rawhide is Alex Wright, a man she's already connected with outside the lifestyle. Can Alex free her from the past and give her the life she longs for?

Bite the Bullet

Montana Steele hopes her new job is a new start. At Rawhide, she'll find willing subs to fit neatly into one compartment of her life. Clint Chavez, part owner of Rawhide, is determined to avoid an emotional relationship. Neither expected the fireworks that erupted between them, nor the erotic attraction that would bind them together despite their best efforts.

Buckskins, Boots & Bondage

Twins Justin and Tucker Davis want one thing—a woman to share for the rest of their lives. Angel Cruz wants two men who'll cherish her forever. Sex between them is hotter than the Texas sun as they play out their fantasies at Rawhide. But when her job threatens their livelihood, will their newfound connection be strong enough to survive?

Master Lovers: Six Stories of BDSM Love

His for the Weekend by Marie Tuhart

Cassie Adams is done with domineering men, yet she's drawn to strong, virile Marcus DeLuca. To get him out of her system, she agrees to be his for a weekend. Marcus wants Cassie in his life, but he senses a secret that keeps her from committing—or submitting—to any man. Can his special brand of domination free her and make her his forever?

Exceeding Boundaries by Mia Downing

Megan Connors needs a man who can make her forget the past. Her boss is a confirmed player and perfect for the job. Adam Wentworth wants Megan, but his preference for dominance holds him back. Will the past keep her bound, or can he convince her she's strong enough to submit?

Legally Bound by Rynne Raines

For years, Domme Eve Morgan has denied her craving for sexual domination. Revealing the truth isn't worth destroying her reputation as a legal shark. Donavan Carver doesn't buy it. To put his doubts to rest, she lures him into a bet he can't win. So what if she cheats? He'll never find out. Or will he?

Buckskins, Boots & Bondage by Desiree Holt

Twins Justin and Tucker Davis want one thing—a woman to share for the rest of their lives. Angel Cruz wants two men who'll cherish her forever. Sex between them is hotter than the Texas sun as they play out their fantasies at Rawhide. But when her job threatens their livelihood, will their newfound connection be strong enough to survive?

Red & Her Big Bad Dom by Sydney St. Claire

Graham Winters loves a woman who won't give him a chance. When he encounters her at a fairytale event at Pleasure Manor, he dons a mask and becomes The Wolf. Lucy Sanchez is attracted to Graham but has a no geek dating rule. Besides, now that she's tasted the pleasures her big, bad Dom offers, how can this Little Red Riding Hood ever go back to vanilla?

At His Command by Felicia Forella

After years of emotional submission to a controlling ex, Julia Stone is wary of a hot young executive with a healthy appetite for sexual dominance. A chance encounter with Julia challenges the Dom in Dalton Fairchild. Can he convince her that submission is the ultimate power?

Lightning Source UK Ltd.
Milton Keynes UK
UKHW020643080321
379980UK00015B/2179